DIRE SALVATION

by
Charles B. Neff

B&H Bennett &
Hastings Publishing

Edited by Adam Finley

ISBN: 978-1-934733-75-2, paperback

For Roger and Nancy Page
And the other dedicated professionals at
Island Books, Mercer Island
"Keepers of the Flame"

DIRE SALVATION

Charles B. Neff

In the following pages you will meet:

Phil Bianchi, Mayor of Swiftwater and Portal, Washington

Jason Ferris, a suspected drug dealer

Calla Ogden, a social worker in Kittinach County, Washington

Greg Takarchuk, a police officer in Swiftwater and Portal

Harland and Janice Casey, volunteers at the Swiftwater Fish Hatchery

Tom Cisek, Chief of Police, Swiftwater and Portal

Sam Espy and Bill McHugh, detectives in the sheriff's office, Kittinach County

Olga Kirilenko, Greg Takarchuk's girlfriend

Lonny Ogden, Calla Ogden's brother

Gabby Thibodeau, night watchman at the Swiftwater Fish Hatchery

DAY ONE

5:52 AM

Lonny in trouble! Calla Ogden snatched off the eyeshade and sat bolt upright, sure that she'd overslept. Bright sunlight glared around the edges of drawn blinds, but the clock read only a few minutes before 6:00 am. She might have slept four hours. More likely three.

The phone call after midnight was still audible in her brain. Her half-brother, Lonny, was in custody. That news alone would have been disturbing, but not unexpected. The twenty-three-year-old, fourteen years her junior, had had numerous brushes with the law. But the words of the neutral-sounding police clerk who'd woken her echoed in her mind: possible involvement in a suspicious death. Lonny had stolen once or twice, been drunk in public a few times. But suspicious death? She knew the term well enough, but what did it actually mean now? Some tie-in with Lonny's occasional drug use? Or, worst case, assault or even murder? Lonny had never come close to anything like that.

She didn't have time to hang around in bed. She'd have to rearrange everything last minute. She hated doing that. Calla swung her legs out, rose, and got dressed, thinking about the day ahead.

First, she had to call her lawyer, Sonia D'Amico. Then she should inform her boss in county social services about what had happened.

Today, luckily, she didn't have a regular schedule. She was leading a hike for The Native Plant Society, of which she was an active member. Their regular leader was visiting his niece in the hospital in Portland, a half-day drive away. If she cancelled, no one else could take her place. People driving in from other parts of the state, wanting to take part in the hike, might already be on the road.

Calla couldn't imagine how she would describe plants, their history and uses, and patiently help strangers look for them. She didn't want to do it. She'd be bad at the task, her mind elsewhere. Yet she could see no alternative but to go through with the responsibility.

That burden again. Accepting responsibility was built into her, by nature or by circumstance, or both. She took care of Lonny and of others too, and tried not to let any of them down.

She ate a single piece of toast with nothing on it. Not because she wanted food, but because she would need energy to get through the day. She fussed around in the second bedroom—her home office with the couch that Lonny slept on when he visited. At 7:00, she called Sonia, who answered her phone, sounding impatient as always but, underneath her grudging tone, willing to help. They agreed to meet at Sonia's office at 7:30.

Calla got there on time. Sonia was dressed for a court date later in the day, wearing a simple brown suit that matched her straight brown hair. Her attire was within the limit of what was considered formal for the Central Cascades, well short of the severe corporate look that locals associated with the go-go western side of the state, Seattle and its urban sprawl.

Calla went straight to the point.

"What's Lonny's situation?"

Sonia replied at a speed just short of brusque.

"Lonny's being held in Swiftwater as a person of interest, but I think he'll be a county case and he'll eventually be transferred to the county jail in Esterhill. They'll question him in a couple of hours. I've rearranged my schedule to be there. Go ahead with your plant walk. You can see him mid-afternoon, I'm guessing."

That was Sonia. Competent and cool. No greeting, and little to indicate concern beyond what was required by law. Except for the look in her eyes. Calla read in them the concern of a friend.

What did Sonia see? Calla's half Indian, half Czech heritage, the dark eyes and black hair of her Native American mother in a round Slavic face? The light brown skin and the feminine, but sturdy, body gifted her by generations of coal miners? Or did she primarily see the sloped shoulders and exhausted face of a hardworking, overburdened woman, stunned and almost felled by bad news about a damaged brother she had worked so hard to keep out of trouble?

As Sonia packed her briefcase, Calla's thoughts returned to the home office in her apartment, the room where Lonny slept on visits. Earlier, she had aimlessly shifted papers on her desk and native figurines on top of the bookcase, as if some tiny change in their location could bring back the security of general order in her life. She visualized Lonny in the room, content and asleep on the couch, even though she never knew when he would show up.

This time, Calla thought as Sonia prepared to leave, it was worse: Lonny might never sleep in that room again.

6:30 AM

Greg Takarchuk sipped his morning tea and realized again how glad he was to be in his new one-bedroom apartment. He could have gone on living with his mother, still grieving over the violent death of his father. But trying that arrangement for a couple of months convinced him that if he wanted to make a go of his career as a police officer, he had to make a break from the mental intrusions of his old home. Besides, in his absence, his mother had begun to form a new life for herself with the community of Ukrainian immigrants to which they both belonged.

Greg stretched his lanky frame, ideal for a basketball player but cramped in a normal bed. He resolved to buy a longer one soon. Also, rugs and pictures for the walls. On his bedside table, the glass in the framed photo of a blond young lady reflected his amber eyes and ginger-colored hair in early-morning disarray.

His feet had just hit the floor when his cell phone rang. He tapped on and immediately heard the voice of Tom Cisek, chief of police for Swiftwater and Portal.

"A dead body has been found. Young male, Caucasian. The body was on county land, but close to our jurisdiction. Just in case someone from our area may be involved, I want you to sit in on the preliminary investigation. Then we'll see whether you can drop out. Come to the office as usual, but keep your schedule open."

Greg acknowledged, tapped off, and sat down for a hasty breakfast at his kitchen table. He knew that the comfortable routine of a small-town police department was bound to be broken from time to time, though suspicious deaths and violent crime were rare in this mountain community. This new one was the first suspicious death since his father had been killed nine months ago. Greg looked forward to working on the case but, depending on how involved he became, he might find himself in a difficult bind.

Last night, Olga, the woman in his bedside picture, had called from Egypt where she was working as a translator. He touched the picture, as if such a simple gesture could magically make her appear beside him, solving just as easily the dilemma he faced. In her call, she'd excitedly announced that she might travel to the States for a training session in one week, and hoped to include a long weekend with him. He wanted very much to be with her; but as a junior police officer he would be in no position to take time off from an active investigation, if the new case went on that long and he was still involved.

Last night, he had hoped that Olga's visit would provide both of them with a chance to figure out their future. Now, the immediate need for him to concentrate on this new case threatened to rise up like a distraction—or worse, like a wall. Would it make sense for her to come at all?

He hurried to put on his uniform, trying to move Olga out of his mind. That was not easy: two other pictures of her looked back at him from a window sill. He pulled his eyes away from her image, reminding himself that the new case before him might be the one to cement his future with the department, ending the scrutiny he was undergoing as a newcomer with only a year and a half of on-duty experience.

As he strode out the door toward his car, the new investigation was foremost in his thinking. But behind it he could still hear concerns about Olga, simultaneously warming and warning him, whirring softly in the background.

7:16 AM

Jason Ferris sat in front of his computer's dual monitor display, willing himself to ignore the bright, darting movement that flashed before his eyes. Four split screens filled each monitor, all eight recording data at different rates, columns of numbers running by too fast to read. With a click, he could access another four screens, then others behind those.

There was a lot more traffic than usual at this time of the morning. But, as always when unexpected events caused complications, Jason stilled everything, bringing his senses as close to suspended animation as he could will them. When his brain and body approached a kind of stasis, a new order would form. Then he would act.

Answers took time, so he pulled back from blankness just enough to allow an infrequent moment of self-analysis, a practice he had all but given up as useless long ago. When he did reflect, it was with a combination of contempt and bemusement: contempt for what he had once been, and bemusement for the pathetic nature of those who thought they could dominate him.

Aaron's Lake, where he had grown up, and the tight little community of souls who clustered within it flickered like a dim movie in front of him. His father the patriarch, already old when Jason was born, held his usual place in the center of the frame. From one hand hung a broad leather belt, its business end, a big brass buckle, swinging gently, deceptively, below. Jason couldn't make out his siblings—some older, others younger. But he knew they would be there, huddling as ordered in a tight semi-circle. They were born so close together that they always seemed, in his memory, to be the same age, all tow-headed, just like him. Scrawny, wearing the same wild and frightened look. Who was the target this time? The next question on all their minds was how loud the old man would scream about righteousness. He never stopped preaching at them, warning them of sin, exalting himself for protecting his children from its ravages. The louder he yelled, the more he lost track of the belt and how long he had swung it.

It was in those moments that Jason discovered the skill of disappearing, finding a way to erase consciousness when bad things happened. Later he would figure out if it had been his turn by counting the welts and bruises on his body. By counting them exactly and making a mental record of the number each time, he discovered that he was able to remember the numbers, all of them. He could move them around and form them into combinations without having to write them down.

As he examined this flickering memory, the other kids appeared, but had no faces. In fact, he'd erased all details about them. Only two names stuck with him: Lila and Nate, and he had no idea what had become of them. They were the weak ones. He was strong. Their bodies were balsa sticks while he was made of hardwood—thin, yes, but tough. He got more beatings than the others, but he could take more, too. When he grew old enough and strong enough to deal with the old man, he was ready. He had liked the way the chair splintered on the old man's back right in the middle of one of his sermons. The preacher was barely alive when Jason left him lying there and, taking with him nothing more than his thirteen years of experience, walked away.

Jason snapped back to his quiet, meticulously clean house and streaming data. His foray into the past had, as always, gained him nothing, except in this case letting necessary information accumulate on the computer. He allowed his consciousness to expand enough to take in part of the data in front of him. One person dead. There were frequent deaths in the meth business. Usually he knew why. Not this time.

He considered his options. Stay put? This place was well known; he'd set it up that way. Visitors wouldn't find anything important. Or he could go to his other place. They had no idea where it was. Get started now and he could be well on his way to Montana, to his cabin and his hog. He wouldn't mind a few days riding back roads on the custom bike. But he'd have to choose fast, if he wanted a choice at all.

The cops would be coming soon; and wherever he chose to be, they'd go on looking for him.

8:11 AM

In the kitchen of his hillside house, Phil Bianchi fixed a simple, healthful breakfast. His fifty-second birthday was just around the corner and, with each new year, Phil became increasingly mindful of photographs of his Italian relatives who had come here to work in the coal mines. The photos recorded their morph from stocky to portly in their old ages. He didn't want to be like that. His wide body had some height to go with it and, with regular exercise, he'd managed to keep close to his college basketball-playing weight. His thick black hair may have receded, leaving a broad half-dome above bushy eyebrows; but from a mirror, clear blue eyes looked back at him out of a still-smooth face.

A half hour later he left the house. His seven-year-old Saab all but drove itself down the hill, past Main Street, lined by nearly all of Swiftwater's businesses. As usual, Main Street had more traffic on it than one might have expected for a town that size, or for the time of day. That was because Swiftwater had Interstate exits on both ends, and travelers often chose the Main Street by-pass to get gas or cabin provisions at the large Safeway.

After working as a journalist in several cities, Phil had returned to the town of his birth as editor of the local paper. That was the year he bought the Saab. When his wife died a year later, leaving him with sadness and lethargy, friends had pushed him into running for mayor. Surprisingly, he had won; and he'd been shepherding—if you could call it that—a town of 5,000 ever since.

The Swiftwater Mayor's job was what you made it. Not full-time, but more than honorific. Swiftwater was too small to justify a professional city manager, and much of the city's business got done, as it always had, when the leading businessmen got together for morning coffee at a back table in the Sunset Café. Phil found himself most busy when disputes arose that wouldn't yield to an informal solution. He was a trained fact-checker and had grown into an effective arbitrator. As to the rest of his job, he could pretty much pick and choose when to add the mayoral presence to festivals, celebrations and other community functions.

When he lifted his eyes, they followed the ridge of the surrounding Cascade Mountains. After a few days of overcast, the sun was fully out, brightening a clear mid-June day, promising the high seventies and daylight until 9:00 pm.

Today should be relaxing and uneventful. No pressing business. He would welcome middle school pupils to a tour of the local fish hatchery, then join a group hiking above Portal to hunt for native plants. He told himself that part of a mayor's job was to get to know the territory; and, while that was true, mostly he liked the excuse for fresh air and exercise.

After two miles, he came to a sign for the hatchery and turned left onto a road that was at once broader and smoother. Though he had probably looked into the matter once, he would have been at a loss to say whether the difference was due to his leaving a county road for a state road or a state road for federal property.

Passing a few outbuildings, he reached a generous parking area with a few cars scattered through it. One section, still empty, was reserved for tour busses. Further on, he saw a traffic barrier and a sliding gate in a ten-foot chain link fence. Long roofs that peaked above the fence belonged to the main buildings where the operations, research, and administration of the hatchery took place.

The hatchery was run by the Yakama Indian Tribe with support from the county, the state, and the federal Bureau of Indian Affairs. As mayor, he had no responsibility for the site, but he enjoyed visiting it and wished the operations he did supervise could all be run as diligently and efficiently as the Yakama cared for the salmon.

Behind a well-tended lawn at the side of the parking lot stood a modest but sturdy structure with a "Visitors' Center" sign over the door. Off to its left was a smaller building, little more than an oversized hut. A frail female figure sat on an orange, four-wheeled cart at the edge of the lawn, leaning to one side to pull weeds out of surrounding flower beds.

He called out.

"Hi. I'm here to meet the middle school visitors."

The woman looked back quickly, put aside a trowel and gloves, and rose from the cart. Her maneuver was slow and contorted; he understood why when he saw that one of her hands gripped a forearm crutch. He briskly closed the distance between them.

She was probably not tall to begin with, and lost more height in a noticeable hunch toward the crutch on her left side. At first he could only see wispy brown hair shot through with gray. As she leveled her gaze at him, he saw a tired, weathered face one click short of haggard, and wide-spaced dusty brown eyes with some challenge left in them. But mostly he recorded the resigned look of someone who lived with daily pain. Her dress was a plain gray-green cotton shift which she tried to smooth with her free hand.

The words from her pinched mouth were calm and surprisingly resonant.

"No busses yet, but they should be here any moment. I just tend the grounds. If you want to know about anything else, you'll have to ask my husband. I'm Janice."

He extended his hand and she responded with a strong grip. In the ensuing silence he did what he had learned most elected officials do by default—he filled it.

"I've been here before. Never saw you and your husband, though. Are you visiting volunteers?"

He really didn't need to ask, since he was well aware of the program. Volunteers could sign up online for various short-term assignments across the United States. Almost always retirees, they contributed labor in some form in return for a small payment. The majority arrived with an RV or a towed trailer. Phil had already spotted the trailer that belonged to Janice and her husband. It filled a space beyond the parking lot and was hooked up to water and sewage connections that rose from a concrete pad.

The trailer was large, but not supersize. One large panel pulled out to form a lateral extension of the interior. On the roof were ladders and a small rowboat. By its side, a 4X4 Toyota pickup stood ready for trips to town, and to haul the trailer when its owners were ready to move on.

Janice waited while his attention swung toward the trailer and back.

"Yes, volunteering for a little while. That's our home, not just transport. Goes wherever we go."

"So where is that?"

Janice amiably held up her end.

"All over. South in the winter, north in the summer. Most of the volunteer jobs are for about a month, two tops."

She focused on something beyond his shoulder.

Phil turned to see a man approaching. Thin and tall with an erect, almost military posture, his long-striding gait ate up the ground. Khaki pants and matching shirt could have been a uniform, except that the man wore no insignia and his shirt was partially unbuttoned to reveal a white T-shirt underneath. Sunlight glinted off a bald head surrounded by a remaining circle of reddish-gray hair. The man began speaking from a mouth full of strong, white teeth before he reached them, his right hand extended.

"Harland Casey at your service call me Harland I see you've already met the better half you must be Mayor Bianchi actually I recognize you from your picture it's an honor to have you among us for as long as your schedule allows hope you can stay as long as possible we've got a lot going on here that we want the world to know about why don't you let me show you around until the kiddies arrive?"

The word torrent stopped and they shook hands. Harland swayed expectantly, beaming. Out of the corner of his eye, he saw Janice recede a step, letting her body slump.

Phil had a good idea of what was going on at the hatchery this time of year. He'd seen before the big, temperature-controlled holding tanks, and could picture at least one of them filled with lethargic salmon, exhausted by their journey from the ocean, up the Columbia River to another hatchery 35 miles away, from which a portion of them had been trucked to this research and supplementation facility. Males and females had already been separated, and semen captured from the males. Following a carefully-monitored matrix, the semen would be released to wild females with a specific genetic make-up. The hatchery operation's most important task was to prevent inbreeding, ensuring fish tough enough to survive the open ocean and the long trip back.

"Thanks, I think I'll just wait on that bench over there. Enjoy the morning sun."

Harland swayed harder.

"You'd be surprised at the changes they've made, even since last year. It's always good to stay up to date."

"Good point. Next time you can take me around."

"It wouldn't take much time. I'll be quick."

Though he was a volunteer and meant well, Harland was getting on Phil's nerves, like the dog in a friend's home who's cute at first with his moist, waggy attention, and becomes a pest when he won't stop. Phil managed a weak smile and, as he walked away, gave Harland a casual hand wave that he tried to make into a signal of thanks more than dismissal.

Two school busses rounded the corner and turned into the parking lot. Sixty or so students spilled out. They traipsed and slouched across the lawn, a squawking gaggle of sparkling, darting eyes and gestures, of cell phones held to up show the latest picture. But as soon as Phil was introduced, they settled down and tried to pay attention. He was being kind to himself as much as to them when he cut in half what he'd planned to say.

Ten minutes later, his Saab was pulling out of the parking lot. Janice Casey was back on her cart, one hand full of weeds. She waved tentatively with the other. Harland, rather stiffly planted by the Visitors' Center, moved his head from side to side as if searching for customers. When his scan took in Phil's departing car, his posture galvanized into an enthusiastic salute.

9:40 AM

Calla waited in her RAV4 in the parking space closest to home plate on the big baseball field. That was the designated meeting point for those who would join her on the plant hike. The field lay in Portal's sole park, if you didn't count the cemetery. Beyond that field were smaller ones for softball and soccer.

Others, especially outsiders, might discount the cemetery, but she'd gone there a half hour ago, on her way to the ball park, to place flowers on the grave of the father she'd never known. He had died from a brain tumor before she was born, but he knew she was coming.

It was strange for her to realize that a part of her had started in this coal town. She could acknowledge her genetic link to it, but otherwise found nothing that touched her in a place she'd first visited only eight years ago. It was so utterly different from the Pitpit reservation where she grew up. Yet Portal was as much in her blood as the reservation: the two parts that made her what she was. All her life she had lived in between them.

She had chosen an apartment on the edge of the Yakama Indian Reservation but spent most of her waking hours in the outskirts of the larger society that surrounded it. When she shopped at the reservation store, stopped for coffee with tribal members, or attended one of the ritual celebrations, she felt included, comfortable, and, in a sense that was difficult to explain to anyone outside that culture, at peace. In the larger culture of rural Washington State, she was needed and useful, her intellectual skills engaged. But she also felt like an outsider in her own land and, at an almost imperceptible level, always on guard.

The crunching sound of a vehicle's tires brought her back to where she sat. An SUV with a Seattle parking sticker on its side window pulled in beside her, and a family of two adults and two teenage boys spilled out. She introduced herself. As they chatted, two more cars appeared: a dusty brown two-door and a large-cab pickup. She identified the young couple from the two-door as the experienced hikers from Leavenworth she had been told to expect. The pickup would belong to a family from Esterhill: a hay farmer, his wife and daughter. Five minutes later an older European car swung into an empty parking place and its driver jumped out with a sheepish grin on his face.

"Sorry to be late. Always one more phone call someone thinks is important. But my phone's turned off now for the next few hours."

The title "mayor" had sounded like a substitute for "tenderfoot" when Calla first heard who was coming along, and she wasn't looking forward to coddling a public official on top of everything else swirling in her mind. She'd met plenty of bureaucrats who were a pain. She knew vaguely of Mayor Bianchi, had attended a few meetings where he spoke, but she had no real idea of him as a person.

Though he was moderately tall, her first impression was of how broad he was through the chest and shoulders. He wore good quality, well-worn boots on the sturdy legs that showed beneath his shorts. Under a wide-brimmed tan hat, he had a nice smile and inquisitive blue eyes, so maybe he wouldn't be a drag on the group or on her dwindling mental resources.

At her suggestion the group left three of the vehicles where they were and piled into her RAV4 and the SUV. She made sure each person had their day pack, lunch, and water bottles. The gently-rising drive to Coho Corner took them past a lake along which houses gradually became less frequent until they totally disappeared. Twenty minutes later they were parked.

Coho Corner was a trailhead location consisting of a large parking area, an infrequently staffed ranger sub-station, and a substantial log building built a century ago when a mining company thought it had discovered riches in the Cascades. From Coho, a network of trails continued west and north deep into the high mountains.

For almost an hour, she led the group along a trail that was at first crowded between tall firs. Narrow as it was, the trail was like a spiritual highway for her. Nature in all its forms was fundamental to Native culture, and when she was outdoors she could almost feel herself open and expand. In other circumstances, her spirits would have flown with the hawks and eagles she knew were up there above the trees. She would have found joy in the colors of the trumpet honeysuckle, trillium, and lupine that peeked coyly from the green undergrowth. Especially the lupine, shaped like purple arrows pointing upward toward the blue sky. But worries about Lonny kept her eyes locked on the rocky path.

As the trail steepened, the trees and undergrowth grew sparse and the hikers gained views of rock escarpments above them, she was relieved to see that everyone in the group was a good hiker, including the mayor, who strode along right behind her. When they reached a place where the trail flattened out and widened, she signaled a stop at a circle of logs that had been laid out to one side.

She sloughed off her pack and waved toward the log circle.

"Here's where we'll start and where we'll return for lunch. You can see over there the trail that goes deeper into the woods. It's a loop we'll follow to look for plants."

For the next hour they moved slowly while she pointed out particular plants, especially rare and endangered ones. She heard her voice almost as an outsider would, and felt the strange disconnect of talking on auto pilot. Questions from the other hikers materialized like apparitions. She heard herself asking for them to be repeated, and registered her attempts to form adequate answers. She hoped no one noticed.

She thought constantly of Lonny and wished that he were there beside her—a different Lonny from the one who languished in jail. They both loved the native plants; Lonny, when he was younger, had spent many enjoyable days hunting them with her. Curiously, the young, inarticulate boy had an instant affinity for plants. He couldn't repeat the names but knew exactly which plant she meant when she called it by any of its names—native, local, or scientific.

At lunch time, she surfaced long enough to see how her group was doing. The couple from Leavenworth wanted to explore farther. They promised to return in a half hour to the log circle where the rest gathered. The teenagers huddled over sandwiches while their parents chatted amiably nearby. Mayor Bianchi—Phil, as he insisted on being called—reviewed notes in what she recognized as a reporter's notebook, an unopened brown lunch bag at his feet. She took her own lunch to the empty log beside him. He glanced at her.

She hardly tasted her food. She had to get to Lonny. She wished the young couple had not gone off exploring. She wanted to leave as soon as possible.

A voice startled her. She pulled herself together enough to realize it belonged to the mayor, and dipped her head apologetically. He spoke again.

"As I said, none of my business, but something seems to be bothering you. I hope it's not serious."

So everything she'd tried to cover up had been obvious.

"I hope not, but probably so. My younger brother's being held in the Swiftwater jail."

"If it's just for a prank or he had too much to drink, he'll be okay, maybe learn a lesson."

At least Phil was sympathetic. She didn't really think about saying more; it just came out.

"Someone died and the police think Lonny is somehow connected to the death."

"That's another matter."

She watched his face stiffen, turn official. So much for sympathy. The resentment that she rarely let show, but that she knew was now mixed with her fear for Lonny, poked through.

"He's Native American. Indian. We're from the Pitpit band—you know, "chick". The small group that was part of the Yakama Treaty but settled on its own reservation. Not very well known."

She heard her defensive tone and didn't like the sound of it. His reply sounded stiff, too.

"That's not an issue in his safety or the way he'll be treated. We have a good record of fairness in our law enforcement departments."

The conversation halted. She felt she should have kept quiet. She'd said too much to a stranger. She was sure their exchange was over, but Phil spoke again.

"If I were you, I'd be worried, too. I can't do anything directly, but I could check on your brother's status and let you know what I find out, if that would help. Lonny Ogden, same last name as yours?"

She nodded. After another briefer pause, he went on, this time in a gentle voice.

"Nothing's harder than having someone you care for in danger. Speaking for myself—and I bet for the others if they knew—I'm grateful for what you taught us today, knowing now that you have so much else on your mind. Another person might have cancelled the excursion."

She looked at the ground but managed half a smile.

"I almost did."

He looked at his watch.

"Time to go. You sit here. I'll round up the others. If you're willing, write down your telephone number and stick it in my pack. I might be able to find out something for you."

She watched Phil encourage the others to get ready to leave. The two hikers from Leavenworth made it easy, returning right on time. Phil showed a politician's skill, using everyone's first name, swapping comments and light jokes, getting people organized and ready to move without being obvious.

To her surprise, she found herself appreciating—at least partly— the side of Phil that had made her suspicious just a few minutes ago. It wasn't much, but even that small lift kept her from sinking deeper into her darkest thoughts.

12:35 PM

Greg Takarchuk waited for the two detectives to arrive. He'd spent the morning in Swiftwater tending to routine business, waiting for a call from the sheriff's office in Esterhill. Swiftwater police covered the cities of Swiftwater and Portal, which, though geographically separate, were incorporated as a single municipality. The sheriff covered everything in Kittinach County that was unincorporated. When a crime overlapped jurisdictions, the sheriff and municipal police worked together on initial investigations.

Tom Cisek, the police chief in Swiftwater, had reminded him of this arrangement when Greg first reached the station, just before 8:00 a.m.

"We've got a suspect in custody and are holding him here for the time being. You'll be working with the sheriff's people. You know the rules. Be available. Do what they ask, unless they ask for too much. Then call me. And remember, cooperating doesn't mean taking over. Follow their lead."

As usual, the reminder didn't take the Chief very long. Same for any discussion of official business, for that matter. When he had his official hat on, Tom Cisek was terse and to the point, scowling at what he thought of as digressions.

Around sixty, he was fit, though stretching his uniform a bit, and broad through the chest over surprisingly short legs. He sat erect in a wooden swivel chair; when he spoke, he looked directly at visitors across a desk that was bare of everything but a plain water glass holding pen and pencils, and a file folder bearing on the topic under discussion. This morning the folder held a single piece of paper.

Greg had nodded as Cisek went on.

"First indications are that the deceased male may have died from a drug overdose. 'Course we got drug-related crime all over, but I'm particularly interested if there's something new—a new drug out there, or a bad batch of an old one. Especially if the source of that stuff could be in this jurisdiction. Otherwise, just help out. We've got enough of a load without adding to it."

The call from Kittinach had come just after lunch and Greg had driven the thirty minutes to Esterhill. The sheriff and his staff occupied a functional metal building with a big parking area at the edge of the city, slightly set off from the motels and car dealerships that lined the city entrance off the Interstate. A receptionist had directed him to an empty conference room and offered coffee. He'd been waiting about ten minutes when the door opened and two men walked in.

They were in plain clothes: jeans for both, a blue shirt for one, a maroon pullover for the other. Big men, both with dark hair, medium length. They looked to be in their late thirties or early forties. At a distance and in loose clothes, it would have been difficult to tell them apart. But one's brown eyes were darker than his partner's, and so was his skin. The darker man's shoulders were broader and his large hands hinted at arms to match. He wore no glasses; the other man did.

Glasses spoke first, probably identifying himself as the senior. His words came out in a soft monotone as he gestured toward his partner.

"I'm Detective Sam Espy. This is Bill McHugh, also a detective in the sheriff's office. I guess you're Takarchuk. Did I say that right?"

"Close enough. Call me Greg. What've we got?"

Espy glanced at McHugh, who flexed his large shoulders, sat, and started right in while he and Espy took other chairs around the table. McHugh's voice was deep, with a growl that Greg thought might have been added for effect. He sat ramrod stiff, his chair angled at Espy though his remarks were aimed at Greg.

"A male body was found about 1.3 miles south of the Swiftwater line in Kittinach jurisdiction. Detective Espy and I made preliminary visits to the site. You'll probably want to take a look on your way back. No gun or knife wounds, no signs of beating or strangulation. Possible drug overdose. The coroner's doing an autopsy now. There are some indications another person was at the site prior to the death. He's being held in connection with the death until we know the facts. The deceased has been identified as Erskine Rolf, early twenties, known as 'Sonny', and he definitely exhibited signs of prior drug use."

Espy picked up the thread, his relaxed posture and higher-pitched tone a marked contrast to McHugh.

"You can't be in police work around here, Greg, without running into meth labs and meth-related crime. I'm assuming you have."

Greg nodded, but wanted to be sure his meaning was clear.

"I've learned a lot from fellow officers. Up to now, though, I've had no direct involvement with meth cases."

Espy and McHugh exchanged a long look. When Espy returned his attention to Greg, a look of resignation was there.

"We don't have time to bring you up to speed on all the players, but we do need help and we'll give you enough to get started."

Greg kept apology out of his voice, simply stating a fact.

"I'm the guy who was available."

Espy stared at him for a moment longer, and brought his expression back to neutral.

"As Bill said, you ought to visit the site. And there's one more task in Portal."

Another glance between the two men. McHugh asked the question, now staring unblinkingly at him.

"Ever heard of Jason Ferris?"

Greg shook his head.

"Not even the name."

Espy took over again.

"That's surprising. He's notorious. But maybe only with people who deal a lot with drugs, mainly meth."

Greg now couldn't mistake the fact that he was being sized up. Espy went on.

"There hasn't been a meth investigation over the last two years, maybe longer, that hasn't looked at Ferris at least once. But we've never been able to pin anything on him. Couldn't even find him, a couple of times."

"Couldn't find him?"

"He's smart and he's slick. Number one, he's got several places. That's our guess, though we only know about one for sure. Number two, he's always informed, like he knows we're coming. Number three, he's got good cover. He claims to be making all his money from internet sales. You've seen the ads. You know, work just a few hours and make a million dollars a week. He's either very good at those sales or he's got another source of income. We think the ball's under cup number two, but so far we haven't been able to prove a damn thing. See what you can find out. If you can find Ferris at all."

Espy tore a page from the small notebook, wrote quickly and handed the page to him. Greg scanned a Portal address and nodded.

The three men rose together. Espy left quickly and McHugh held back.

"This Ferris, be careful."

McHugh was giving him more than a casual warning, standing in close, using proximity like a command. Nothing new there. In Ukraine you grew up with street toughs, and on the basketball court in Swiftwater you always expected the biggest guy on the opposing team to do or say something intimidating even before the first toss-up. Greg gave no ground and, his eyes level with the detective's, stared right back at dark eyes that held an expression he recognized. They weren't after control, but dominance. Greg didn't want a fight, but he was not about to back down.

"He's dangerous?"

McHugh didn't move. Greg could almost feel him swell.

"You have no idea. He controls the drug distribution in this county, and is better than anyone at hiding it. Whatever he tells you will be a lie."

He waited until McHugh waved a hand in dismissal, as if giving up on someone who was incapable of getting it. Meanwhile, he tried to figure out whether the encounter told him more about Ferris or about McHugh.

Probably some of both. But he'd need more information to figure out who each man really was, to decide what was real and what was for show.

2:56 PM

Jason Ferris had made up his mind more than an hour ago: he'd stay put in his little house in Portal. There was no percentage in playing cops and robbers this time. He'd done that often enough to know that he could win without sweating it. Winning so easily took the fun out of the game. Not that winning was ever that much fun. Or fun the object of the game.

At first he eluded the police just to prove to himself that he could do it. Then to prove to them that he could hide for as long as he wanted to. The last few times it had felt like they already got the message, or else they got the message and didn't understand what it meant. Either way, it didn't matter.

Besides, he was as surprised as the police. Normally he could extract from his closely-watched data either positive indications that something was about to happen or enough abnormalities that he was never surprised by an unusual event, like a random dead body. Not this time. Not even a hint.

He sat now in a leather Lay-Z Boy recliner, an iPad on his lap. The device had remained unused for the last twenty minutes. He was getting bored; and if that went on much longer, he'd leave anyway. He picked up the iPad, searching for a distracting idea. At least once a day he dreamed on the pad, letting his mind roam, letting free association guide the sketching wand. When the screen filled with lines, numbers, doodles, he would stop long enough to inspect the results. If he found any unusual connections in the jumble, he would send that image over wi-fi to the printer in the room behind him. That printout went into a document folder where he stored it along with many others he had produced. Later, when he was planning something difficult, he would consult those images. Going through them often helped him find the key to a problem he'd come up against.

This time, nothing unusual showed in his doodling. Leaving was looking better all the time. He let his eyes pass around the bare parlor which held only the recliner, a table and lamp, a TV and a gas fireplace. It didn't provide space for visitors; he never had visitors anyway.

He'd bought this place for next to nothing. His little house had looked worse than most, but he'd checked the important parts: the foundation, framing, and floors. They were solid and mostly true. The rest was easy—a new roof, windows, siding. He'd done all the work himself, even converting the basement into a rudimentary chemistry lab where he'd once done preliminary drug analysis. He still had the analytical capability, but now the shelves were stocked with the products he was currently selling over the internet—diet miracles, salves, gels, teeth whiteners, and other cheap beauty products that promised nirvana to the idiots who would buy them. They were all junk. He needed no analysis to know that.

A knock on the front door, sounding louder than it really was, ripped him away from his mental inventory. He sat absolutely still. From a place deep inside, he waited for more information. His heart rate slowed and his primary senses grew acute, scanning his environment for telltale sounds and smells, or for minute changes in light and shading. Some time passed before he heard the knock again.

He moved silently toward the front wall where he could peer obliquely through the folded vertical slats of the window shutters. He registered a brown hat down to black boots, piecing together the image of a uniformed visitor. He reexamined his earlier decision to stay rather than run, and quickly decided it still was correct. He took three gliding steps to his right and called out.

"Who are you?"

A neutral, conversational voice answered.

"Officer Takarchuk, Swiftwater and Portal Police. Can I talk to you?"

As long as he had decided to stay, better now than with a subpoena. He opened the door a two-inch crack. It wouldn't open any farther until Jason removed three chains, each attached to fasteners on bars across the door.

Still hidden by the two-inch oak door, he addressed the crack.

"What do you want?"

"To talk to Jason Ferris. Is that you?"

The cop's voice remained calm and unhurried.

Jason thought a second. Okay. No games this time.

"Yes."

"Are you aware that a person died under suspicious circumstances last night, not far from here?"

"I watch the news like anyone else."

"So you are aware?"

"Yes. But it has nothing to do with me."

The policeman waited, then continued in a slightly more official tone.

"May I come in? I have a few questions, all routine. We can be done in just a few minutes. Otherwise, I may have to use a more official way to gain entrance and question you."

Jason closed the door and thought hard. He knew the drill. The cop would wait, reinforcements would arrive. He would have to decide whether to agree voluntarily to questioning, or to invite trouble and expense. He could deal with the hassle if he refused the cop's entry. But why put up with it? His mind riffled through several downside possibilities of letting this officer in and found none of them too serious. He slowly unlatched the chains, then opened the door and got a full view of the policeman.

His visitor's left arm now clamped his hat, and Jason saw reddish blond hair and amber eyes regarding him levelly. The man was lean and tall. Jason's eyes were about even with the cop's shoulders, making the policeman around six-four. He was young. Could be they were both close to the same age. The visitor seemed confident without being threatening or authoritative.

The policeman stepped in past Jason and took a position in the middle of the room. Jason felt an uncharacteristic twinge of irritation. He moved quickly to establish who was in charge, flopping down into the recliner.

The cop took a stride toward him, laid a card on the arm of the recliner, and stepped back.

"Again, I am Officer Takarchuk. You'll find my number for future reference on the card."

Jason didn't move a muscle, and Takarchuk went on.

"Can you tell me where you were last night?"

Maybe—though in principle he hated the idea—he ought to give the cop something.

"Right here, all night. Not that it's any of your business."

"We're checking leads, that's all."

"I'm not a lead and you know it. I'm a possibility, a guess. The same guess your department always makes without proof. No difference this time."

The cop just nodded. No crowding closer or raising his voice. Not like that asshole McHugh. This cop at least seemed to think.

"All right. Let's say you were here all night. Can you help me out, give me any proof? I don't want to waste time on you if I don't have to, and I'd guess you'd like to avoid the hassle."

For a second, that stopped Jason. If any cop had ever approached him like that before, he couldn't remember it. Mostly he got pretend courtesies, simple to see through.

"I was alone."

"You said that before."

He had let the cop in and the cop was being respectful enough. But that could change very quickly if he refused to give up anything. He paused, making the cop wait even after he'd made up his mind.

"Okay, Tucker …

He picked up the card off the chair and checked the name.

… *Takarchuk*, I'll give you some information, but I give it to you with a warning. Check your records. About eighteen months ago, your department got a warrant and tore my computers apart. Found nothing. If you do that again, my lawyer has a suit already drawn up."

The cop replied without reaction.

"I'll check our files."

"You better, because I'm about to give you—voluntarily—information that should take me out of your investigation. If you try to get more without probable cause, I'll also file against you personally."

"You know you can't threaten an officer, but I'll accept your statement as one of fact."

Jason was surprised to see the hint of a smile on Takarchuk's lips, though his tone of voice stayed with the seriousness of the moment. The guy was cool, for sure. Jason took his time reviewing what he could gain or lose and made up his mind to go on.

"Here's what you get. I was at my computer until about 2 am. I'll give you an edited version of my work on a thumb drive. You can check the date and time stamps. You might try to say that I accessed my computer from a mobile device, but the volume of entries will prove that I couldn't have done that work *and* been near your dead body at the same time."

"Let's see what you've got. I'm not saying that will be enough. Others have to decide that. How long will it take you to edit your files?"

"I won't give you a full record, just enough to demonstrate when I was online. In an hour I'll have it ready."

"Show me your computer. I need to make sure it's here. Otherwise your printouts prove nothing."

Jason didn't have a choice. But he wasn't going to show much. He rose and strode to the closed door on the back wall.

"Don't blink. You only get one look."

He opened the door wide, counted to three, and closed it. Takarchuk peered over his shoulder, barely having time to take in the essentials: the workspaces along two walls, the massive monitors, the multiple desktop towers, the back-up storage drives, and a narrow bed where Jason slept.

If Takarchuk had any reaction, it didn't show. His voice was utterly calm.

"You'll be here if I return in an hour?"

It was both a question and a statement.

"Why wouldn't I be?"

"I guess some would say…"

Takarchuk let the statement hang, put on his hat, and left by the front door.

Jason waited for the chains to stop rattling, locked up, and went to his computer. Soon he was deep into figuring out the minimum he could give the police.

But a corner of his brain had started thinking about how to stop this bullshit for good.

4:30 PM

Calla sat in the small waiting area at the Swiftwater police station, an area that consisted of just a few seats at a right angle in a rear corner of the entry. An elderly couple occupied the chairs farthest from her, heads down, slung forward in motionless dejection. On the side where she sat a window provided a pass-through for people with judicial business. A solid door, from which her eyes refused to move, faced her. Above the door, a sign announced "Police Department – Official Business Only".

She'd been waiting for over an hour and still there was no indication when she'd be able to see Lonny. Surprisingly, Phil Bianchi had arrived soon after she did. He had come over to offer an encouraging smile and shake hands, then went through the solid door. The secretary behind the reception desk had mentioned that Sonia, her lawyer, was also inside. With no book or magazine to provide distraction, she could do nothing but stare at the sporadic flow of traffic down Main Street, and worry. The longer she waited, the less she noticed the traffic.

She purposely kept her eyes off her watch or the big clock on the wall above her head, so she couldn't tell how long she had been there when Sonia came out and sat beside her.

"Sorry you've had to wait so long, Calla. I know it's tough, but for now there's little we can do. You didn't tell me…"

Sonia looked momentarily apologetic and started over.

"If there's a fault, it's probably mine. I should have asked about Lonny's place of residence. The fact that he seems to live in several places—at your apartment, but also with friends on the reservation, may make him a resident of land administered in part by an Indian tribe. So there's some question about how much BIA and the tribal police need to be involved before his processing can be completed.

That's the main reason for the delay. Don't worry, though, he hasn't been charged with anything. At this point they're just trying to find out where he was last night."

Calla tried to match her lawyer's calm.

"Did you get to see him?"

"Just a few minutes ago and not for long. He had to ask for me as his attorney before I could get access. I got a note in to him about an hour ago, and he did ask for me. Talk about a surprise. I've never thought he liked me. He could change his mind, but I'm officially representing him, at least for now."

"I'm glad of that, but how is he? That's what I really want to know."

Sonia examined Main Street for a moment and spoke carefully.

"Confused, scared. I know he has always had trouble expressing himself, but that was especially true today. Sometimes he wouldn't answer my questions. Lots of his answers made no sense. I still don't know what he was doing last night and I'm not sure that he knows himself. But I do know he's scared."

"But of what?"

"No idea. When I asked him that question, he clammed up."

Sonia craned her neck to look at the big clock.

"Sorry. I've got a 5 o'clock at the office. I'll call you this evening."

Sonia left and Calla wondered whether she shouldn't do the same. She may not even be able to see Lonny today; but if she did, would her presence make any difference to him? She'd never been sure that she made any difference in his life.

Depression licked the edges of her thoughts and she shoved it roughly away. It was time to do what she had always done: pull herself together, fight back. This was a particularly rough patch, but, like all the other rough patches, she'd get through it.

The air around her changed, and she escaped her thoughts enough to record the arrival of someone in the seat next to her. It took a moment more for her to recognize Phil Bianchi. He was watching her with the care of someone gingerly holding a breakable object. His voice echoed the same caution.

"Are you okay?"

"Yes ... no, actually, I'm not sure."

"The wait is hard."

He said that like someone who knew what he was talking about. She nodded. He continued in the same tone.

"I couldn't have seen him either, even if I'd asked. My impression is that they're waiting for more evidence before a preliminary interview."

"More? They have something already?"

Phil kept looking at her thoughtfully.

"I guess it wouldn't hurt to tell you. Lonny was found in his truck, not far from where the body was discovered. They also found a hat that they think might be Lonny's, in the vicinity of the body."

The location of the truck could be bad news, but the hat could be worse.

"Did they describe the hat?"

"I could see it in an evidence bag. Like a ski hat with circles of different colors stacked up. Red, orange, and yellow."

Her heart sank. When Lonny had extra money, he went to a store that sold used clothes and some new seconds. One day he found three hats in the same pattern, one mostly red, one mostly blue, and the third mostly green. Lonny liked these hats so much that he was hardly ever seen without one of them on, regardless of the season.

Phil must have noticed.

"Look. I asked and they told me informally that if Lonny can have visitors, the first time is likely to be later this evening. But it might be tomorrow. No sense waiting right now; waiting on an empty stomach will only make things worse for you. Let's go to Bart's and get something to eat. I know I'm hungry, and would bet you are, too."

He took her elbow and helped her up. She almost shook him off. She could do it on her own. But as she leaned into his arm, she realized that doing so was just helpful, not momentous. She didn't pull away as they walked to his car.

6:41 PM

While waiting once again for Espy and McHugh at the sheriff's office in Esterhill, Greg's mind wandered to his far-away girlfriend

Olga and her plans to visit Swiftwater. He ought to give her a definite answer, but this case was still in the preliminary stages. He might be dismissed in a day or two, not needed once facts had been gathered. But what if he was asked to continue on the case during the time she planned to visit? If that happened, he couldn't refuse. As much as he wanted to give Olga an answer, he just couldn't settle the matter right now.

Instead, he concentrated on what Jason Ferris had given him. From his briefcase, he removed a thin sheaf of printouts, the data Jason had transferred to a thumb drive. They amounted to strings of numbers and symbols around six to eight lines long, each string preceded by a date and time. Greg could navigate a computer well enough, but when it came to really technical issues he was as ignorant as the next guy. He could see that the date was the same—yesterday—for all of the printouts, and the times ranged from 8 pm to about 2:45 am. But what these numbers and symbols meant beyond that, he couldn't say.

He was still scanning the data strings when the door opened and Espy and McHugh came in. He had looked up both men in the department records and now he knew more about them. For one thing, they were not the same age. There was a seven year difference between the two: McHugh was 46 and Espy 39.

McHugh had a BS in Criminology at Central, and had completed part of the requirements for an MA. He had been with the department for eighteen years and had one departmental commendation about ten years ago. He was also experienced in search and rescue and apparently was in demand during rescues in all parts of Central Washington.

Espy had a GED, caught the end of Desert Storm as a raw MP, then worked in Montana and Idaho, getting a college degree along the way, before coming to Kittinach County seven years ago. Though the record did not say so explicitly, Greg guessed that Espy now outranked McHugh; and he had tucked that thought away.

He watched the two men as they sat down. Up close they didn't look that much alike. Espy was slimmer, and showed a slight squint and wrinkles behind his glasses that made him look older than he was.

The burden of responsibility? McHugh's chest and shoulders were over-size and he moved both a lot of the time. Maybe to let you know he was no one to mess with? Greg had also found a notation in the record that identified McHugh as Native American. Now that he saw the man up close, and with that in mind, he did see hints of native features.

Espy led off.

"Bill and I spent most of the afternoon at the location where they found Rolf: the rear of a service station that was closed for the night. Time of death was between half past eleven and 12:30. Rolf was 22, part Hispanic. He grew up in Yakima but lived for five years in Spokane where, according to police, he was into drugs, but nothing major. He had no record. The preliminary tox reports should be ready tomorrow sometime. We also found a physical item that might be worth something. More on that later."

Espy looked up from his notes. McHugh seemed ready to talk, but Espy got in the first question to Greg.

"What did you get?"

"I visited the crime scene on my way here. Didn't find anything of interest beyond what you guys got already."

McHugh hunched forward with a grimace.

"What about that fucker Ferris? I thought that was supposed to be your primary."

Greg let the vehemence wash over him without reacting.

"I was just getting to that. I found him."

McHugh's face went slack for an instant, then returned to anger.

"Found him? We're talking about the same guy? Jason Ferris?"

"He was at the address you gave me. He let me in and we talked."

"Bullshit!"

McHugh turned to Espy for confirmation, but Espy kept his focus on Greg.

"Describe him."

"Five-seven, one-forty, blond short hair, blue eyes. Tries to act calm, but his brain's always in high gear, like he figures he can out-smart you. Hates cops. Plays offense as the best defense."

Espy gave a wry grin.

"That's him. Go on."

Greg summarized Ferris' offer of limited cooperation. As he finished, he laid the computer printouts and the thumb drive on the table in front of Espy.

McHugh made a rude gesture.

"If it's from Ferris, none of that's worth a shit."

Espy leafed through the papers, his head down and his arm by his side. Silence descended. Greg used the time to add to his impression of Espy. McHugh was such a large and overbearing presence, so in your face with his physicality, that Espy could easily seem diminished. Throughout their meetings, Greg noticed that Espy habitually held a pen in his right hand, and while he was thinking something through, he dropped that hand toward the floor, the pen swinging back and forth like the end of a pendulum. He remained cool during McHugh's eruptions, allowing them to wash over him without reacting in return. He also didn't mind showing brief glimpses of an ironic, slightly detached sense of humor.

Espy raised his head and his arm. His pen was back up, hovering over the printout.

"I'm no expert, but I can see what Ferris is doing. Maybe this rules him out, maybe not. We'll see what the experts say."

He shifted to McHugh.

"Bill, go see if our computer guy is still here, or else call him back here."

McHugh stared back grimly, then left the room.

Espy shook his head.

"One of Bill's strengths is that once he gets onto something he won't give it up. One of his weaknesses is that it's hard for him to see when it's time to give up. Sometimes he sounds out of control. But all in all, he's a solid law enforcement officer."

Greg had trouble acknowledging strength in obsession, but no need to get into that. He nodded and moved on.

"What about the physical items you mentioned?"

"You know about our picking up the Indian man, Lonny Ogden. He's in lock-up now. He's not saying much. On the service station property, near the road, we found a hat that might be Lonny's, and closer to the body a wrapper for Swizzlers—you know, those long, twisted licorice or red candies? The one we found was for the licorice type. We asked at the service station and at the only store nearby, but neither place sells that candy. We're checking to see if Rolf was known to favor licorice. And..."

The door opened and McHugh returned. He reported to Espy without sitting down. Greg's hunch that Espy was in charge was confirmed.

"I had to get the duty officer out of the interview room where he was talking to Ogden. He gave me the number of our computer guy and I'll call him now. But he also told me that Ogden said he'd been staying out at the hatchery. Thought you oughta know that."

"Make your call, Bill. Greg, why don't you go out to the hatchery and see if you can find anything useful there? The crew will be gone for the day, but the night watchman should be around."

Greg rose to leave and saw McHugh fire a sour expression in his direction. Missed, he thought. But how long was he going to have to keep an eye on McHugh, when they should be aiming at figuring out the reasons for a suspicious death instead of sniping at each other?

7:16 PM

Phil opened the door for Calla. Bart's restaurant was a new place designed to seem older. Swiftwater, in looking forward, opted for an old-town atmosphere as its best ticket for the future. The pictures on the pine-paneled walls, and the design of booths and tables, matched the exterior used-brick façade, collectively evoking the first decades of the 20th century. A small casino in the rear was far enough away that no noise reached Phil and Calla in the sparsely-filled restaurant.

Calla perked up somewhat after half a glass of iced tea and several bites of an onion-smothered flank steak, but to Phil she still looked pale and tired when she spoke.

"Lonny has never been an easy person and he has his problems. But it's always been kid stuff—trespassing, shoplifting, that kind of thing. I just don't think it's possible that he could be connected to someone's death unless it was some terrible accident that wasn't his fault."

He didn't want to disturb her any further, but the former reporter in him still had a penchant for the tough questions.

"How can you be sure?"

He watched her size him up. In her shoes, he'd be hesitant too. Her eyes slid into a place between resignation and desperation. She needed to talk.

"My mother was a strong person when she raised me. But then she started heavy drinking. Lonny was born with fetal alcohol syndrome. You can see that in his small head and thin upper lip. He's got hearing and coordination problems, and he's never been able to concentrate on anything for long. If he's calm, he can tolerate simple and repetitive activity. If he's stressed or anxious, he's all over the place. When he's like that, he never follows advice, might not even process it. That gets him into trouble sometimes, but his whole life he's managed to stay away from really dangerous situations. You see, Lonny underneath is a gentle soul. He's kind to animals and babies. He's afraid of guns, even shies away from firecrackers, and hates the sight of blood. But that's not what makes me think he couldn't be involved in this death the police are investigating, unless it was an accident."

"Okay then, why not?"

"Because if it was something more than an accident, Lonny would have had to *plan* it. Lonny's no good at planning. He's lost job after job because he couldn't organize even simple tasks. He only manages to hold on to the job at the hatchery—maybe it's gone now—because the people around him organize his tasks for him. So if he was involved in this death somehow, it would have to have been an accident."

Phil thought that over. It was a strong point, but not a perfect one. He wanted to be a supportive listener, but he'd also learned that the truth was the best support in the long run.

"I don't doubt what you say, but if Lonny was at all involved then the police need to hold him until all the facts come out. He may be totally innocent, but then again there is always the chance that Lonny did something wrong, even if it was unintentional or accidental. And then there's the hat."

She had no immediate response. He watched Calla fold into herself. Maybe he'd gone too far with his honesty. She looked so vulnerable that he felt sorry for her. Actually, more than sorry. Protective. Recognizing that reaction in himself was a surprise.

She gave him another surprise with a change of subject.

"What about you? What brought you to Swiftwater? Tell me, take my mind off Lonny."

"Born here. Went away. Came back with a wife who died. I was a journalist who got talked into being mayor."

The hint of a smile almost lit her face.

"That's the text message version. Now how about…"

Her cell phone must have vibrated. She reached for it, listened briefly and reported: she could have her visit with Lonny now.

He drove her back to the police station. Once they were inside the building, Calla was allowed immediate access to the holding area, and Phil got permission to go in in with her. An officer sat in an alcove off a short hallway with two jail cells on each side. The officer checked Calla's ID, consulted a form on his desk, and instructed Calla that she could have ten minutes with her brother in one of the interview rooms, but was not to touch him or give him anything. The officer would wait nearby while they talked.

Phil and Calla sat in chairs that lined one wall while the officer went down the hallway and opened one of the cell doors.

A few minutes later the officer appeared again, his hand on the back of a shambling figure. To Phil it looked as if the officer's hand provided all of the forward propulsion; without its force, Lonny might have collapsed where he stood. His head drooped so Phil could not fully see his face. As for the rest, Lonny had a frail body and sallow brown skin. "Dangerous" would have been one of the last words that he would have used to characterize Calla's brother.

Calla rose and took two fast steps toward her brother, her extended arms ready to embrace him. But she caught herself, and her arms fell to her sides. Lonny gave no sign of acknowledgment as he and the officer passed Calla and entered an interview room. Calla fell in step behind them and the door closed.

Got to get going, Phil thought. Or did he? What was there at home? Nothing of urgency. He'd wait then, and see what happened in the interview room. His presence might be of value, he told himself, though he knew he would be hard-pressed to say why. He spotted a copy of *The Pioneer*, the local weekly, on the officer's desk, retrieved it, and tried to concentrate on what he read until the door opened again.

Lonny exited first, this time with his head up and walking under his own power. He looked blankly ahead, revealing light eyes with dark half-moons below them, active acne, and a mop of thick black hair that looked as if it had been chopped into disorder.

Calla exited a moment later, assuming Lonny's drooping head and listless shuffle. She silently walked toward the exit from the holding area. Phil joined her in the foyer. Down the hallway, he recognized Greg Takarchuk, deep in concentration. The two of them exchanged a perfunctory smile and a wave.

In the parking lot, a faint buzz above them descended from yellowish street lights on high poles. Beyond their glow, touches of fading daylight outlined the mountains.

Calla unlocked her car door and, leaving the door open, turned toward him. The interior light reached the bottom part of her head, so he could see her lips move but couldn't see her eyes.

"Lonny's confused and his story is no help. He claims he went out last evening, had a couple of beers and smoked a joint. He remembers the bar where he had the beers, but is not sure where he had the pot. He met two guys from the bar whose names might have been Jack and Al. He's not sure. He doesn't remember much about leaving the bar except that he was very tired. He drove away in his truck and after a while decided he wouldn't make it to the hatchery. So he pulled over and went to sleep. He was in the truck when the police arrived and arrested him."

"Why the hatchery?"

"Didn't I tell you he was staying at the hatchery? He has a part-time job there and they let him sleep in one of the outbuildings."

"Do you think…?"

He felt her hand on his arm.

"I'm sorry, I can't think any more. Or at all. Just too tired. You've been nice, but I've got to get home."

"Are you up to the forty-minute drive? How about staying at the motel?"

"I can make it."

He put his hand on her shoulder, and that physical contact made him realize that he didn't want Calla to leave. He let habit rescue him with a standard caution.

"Be careful."

She didn't move right away. Then she did, and drove away.

8:55 PM

Greg looked around before getting out of his car. The glow of the half-moon joined the last vestiges of daylight in illuminating the hatchery's empty parking lot. The only vehicle in sight was a truck parked next to a trailer across from the lot, near the gated entrance to the hatchery. Light shone at the edges of the trailer's curtains.

Another light caught his attention, this one moving. A bouncing flashlight, behind which was a figure approaching his car.

He stepped out of the car just as a soft voice called.

"Need help there?"

As a newly-arrived nine year old who had spoken Ukrainian and Russian all his childhood, Greg couldn't detect the varied accents of English. All English speakers initially sounded the same to him. Over the years, he began to pick up on the faster diction of people from Seattle, and spot the family heritage of locals whose relatives still lived in eastern Nevada or Texas, or who were of Hispanic lineage. Visiting tourists from the East Coast became easier to identify. And the soft Native-American accent fixed itself in his hearing.

The native accent was a subtle marker, faintly musical, not quite sing-song, but with a gentle cadence all its own. This man had it.

Greg held up a hand to slow the approaching figure.

"I'm Officer Takarchuk, Swiftwater Police. Can I talk to you?"

The man kept a safe distance.

Greg pulled out his identification and held it at arm's length. The flashlight moved closer.

"Looks okay, I guess. What can I do for you?"

"Maybe we can go where there's more light."

He followed the moving flashlight to an outbuilding by the visitors' center and waited while keys jangled, a door opened, and a light went on. A single room held a table with a computerized projector pointing at a screen on one wall. Other walls exhibited posters and graphs about salmon. Four chairs stood by the table, a white pad and pen in front of each.

The night watchman was scrawny, with forward-curved shoulders that gave him a stooped appearance, though he stood fairly upright. A messy shock of white hair rode above leather-brown skin. He wore cowboy boots, jeans, and a tan work shirt over which hung a too-large jacket of the same color. His dark eyes looked calm, but vigilant. His age was likely in the mid-fifties.

Greg offered his identification again and the man shook his head.

"Saw it okay the first time."

"Could I have your name? I'll need it for my report."

Vigilance in the man's eyes, but no hesitation in the reply.

"Don't see how that could hurt. Gabby Thibodeau. I'll spell it."

The watchman leaned over the table, wrote on a pad in block letters and handed the sheet of paper to him.

"Thank you, Mr. Thibodeau."

Greg gestured toward two chairs. Thibodeau shook his head.

"Rather stand. And I answer best to Gabby. Last name's too hard for most."

"Okay by me, Gabby. You the only one around?"

"Me and that couple in the trailer."

"And who are they?"

"Volunteers from Arizona. Harland and his wife Janice. Nice people, I guess. Hard workers."

"I'll talk to them later. You know Lonny Ogden?"

"Seen him around. Don't really know him. Besides, I'm only here nights."

"But you've met him."

"Once or twice."

"And you know what's happened to him?"

Hesitation and a downward look until Thibodeau raised his head again.

"There's rumor at the rez that the cops arrested him."

"Got any idea why that might be?"

Eyes brimmed with suspicion.

"Why would I?"

Greg decided to regroup. It wasn't the first time he'd been too direct and spooked a possible source. Chief Cisek had gotten on him about that more than once.

"I'm not accusing you of anything. Just asking."

Silence, unwavering eyes.

Greg punctured the silence.

"How about an easy one? Does Lonny like licorice?"

Suspicion faded, replaced by surprise and a smile.

"Why that? You sellin' candy? I got no idea about Lonny and what you say … licorice?"

"That's all right. I'll ask the couple in the trailer. You think they know Lonny?"

"Sure. Everybody knows Lonny. Don't know how well they know him. You'll have to ask 'em."

"I'll do that."

He walked across the center's circular lawn toward the trailer as Thibodeau remained behind to lock the door. Greg climbed the two steps that hung from the trailer's side and knocked. The door opened almost immediately. A tall bald man filled the frame, a vertical index finger against his lip and the other hand held up palm outward. Greg stepped back silently and waited while the door closed and opened again.

The tall man emerged, holding a lit Coleman lantern which emitted a bright, steady light that glinted off a polished metal housing. Silently the man closed the door and led Greg around a parked pickup truck to a picnic table. He placed the lantern at the table's center. That act was like a lever releasing a pent-up torrent of words.

"Harland Casey couldn't speak before the wife's asleep she's got infirmities that make sleepin hard so when she conks out I try to be quiet we can talk here all right and this LED lantern gives us light got it at Costco we go there every week and find good deals like this one."

Greg took an outstretched hand and quickly withdrew from its tightening grip. If those words were any indication, the handshake could have lasted a while. Greg introduced himself and showed his ID. Casey barely glanced at it, keeping his focus on Greg as if he were a servant in waiting. His hands gripped the edge of the table, instantly ready to shove off and follow instructions.

"Thanks for seeing me this late, Mr. Casey. I'm collecting information for an investigation. Do you know a Lonny Ogden?"

"Absolutely he's a native young man who docs light chores for us we see him three or four times a week."

"What kind of chores?"

"Simple clean up checking the grounds for tossed-away papers and garbage although the tourists are pretty careful I suppose we could get along without him but he does relieve me and Janice of stoop work and that's hard for us tall guys and for her with her infirmities and all sometimes we send him to Safeway to get stuff for us and the hatchery people."

Casey stopped for breath and Greg tried to steer him in another direction.

"My understanding is that Lonny stays here at night."

That statement made Casey pause. In the seconds that followed, Greg got the impression that Casey might just have registered the fact that their conversation could be tied to an investigation.

"Is that important?"

Suddenly Casey wasn't quite as chatty.

"Too early to know. Does he or does he not stay here?"

"Only sometimes. We feel sorry for him and it's obvious he's got problems so we ..."

"Show me where he stays."

Casey flashed a brief look of indecision, then shoved off from the table, hoisted the lantern, and led them toward the hatchery.

They walked around the lowered vehicle gate to the chain link fence, which presented another gate, this time a sliding one with a keypad and a large red button beside it. Casey punched in numbers.

"If you hit the button the watchman comes to open up. But the bell's pretty loud and could wake Janice."

To the sound of metal grating on metal, the gate slid open and they entered. Before the gate finished its noisy return, Casey was in full loping stride and Greg had to hurry to stay abreast. They passed long concrete fish tanks and the administrative and research buildings, arriving at a metal shed. Casey pulled on a chain; a segmented door rolled up. The lantern light fell on the front end of a small tractor and on tools hung on the wall. When Casey flipped on a light, Greg could see more equipment plus full, stacked plastic bags and shelves with paints and solvents.

Casey walked to the rear of the shed, where he opened a door and turned on another light.

"Here's where Lonny sleeps when he stays over. Not much, but then he doesn't seem to need much."

"Not much" was an understatement. Immediately in front and to the left of the door entrance hung other hand tools, tarps, and a motley collection of rain gear. That left a bit more than half of a ten-by-four foot space for an uncovered mattress on the floor, with a crumpled quilt at its center. Two cardboard boxes sat on a shelf on the wall above the mattress.

"How did it happen that Lonny got a job here?"

He expected another spate of words in reply, but Casey had calmed down.

"As I recall, he came one day and then returned fairly regularly. Looked real lost. Janice gave him food and talked to him. I guess he had another home but he liked it here. He's at least part Indian, so we talked to the Yakamas who manage the hatchery and they decided to let him do some part-time work, mostly in the summer when it's busy."

"When did all that start?"

"Beginning of summer a year ago."

Casey's appearance had changed. His loopy, forced smile was gone. He stood at ease and his answers were succinct and to the point. Curious, but then again—the presence of a police officer often made people act funny.

"Did you notice that Lonny liked candy?"

"Oh yeah. He has a real sweet tooth. Janice makes him cookies. But he likes candy best."

"Any particular kind?"

"Chocolate chip."

"I meant the candy. How about licorice?"

There was a slight delay in Casey's reply—no more than a hiccup—and a fleeting look of discomfort that he covered with a smile.

"Sure he likes licorice seems more than other candy and Janice laid some in to make him happy when he asked for it which was pretty often unless he found some other kind of candy first."

The motor mouth was back.

"Those boxes up there, can I have a look at them?"

"Anything you want glad to help."

Casey pulled down the first box and handed it to Greg, who lifted the flaps and took a quick look inside, finding a jumble of clothes, most in need of a wash. Greg put the box back and lowered the second one. It contained more clothes, soap, a toothbrush and toothpaste in a baggie.

And two packages of licorice Swizzlers.

10:45 PM

Jason liked the shadowy corner at the back of the bar where he was nursing a Virgin Mary. It was quiet and anonymous, and he could observe without being observed. For him, that was always the best situation.

The roadhouse bar at the start of Blau Pass was not new to him. He'd been here once before—two years, eleven months and six days ago. A Tuesday. Those facts popped up without his searching for them. His mind was never empty of the facts that he needed in any particular moment.

His mind told him, too, that it had been all right to talk to that cop Takarchuk, even to let him into the house. But other parts of him—his heartbeat, a dirty feeling on his skin, unexpected twitching, and occasional lightning-like flashes—all might be saying something different. Maybe they were the "feelings" that the school counselor told him he "needed to be in touch with". But touching them would make him enter a dark space he'd left behind and promised himself he'd never visit again.

A few months ago, he'd noticed that his heart rate was up, but didn't think much about it. Then came the scattered moments of twitching and flashes. It wasn't until after Takarchuk left that they all arrived at the same time, each stronger than before, collectively insistent. Were they a warning? His mind scanned the objective situation and came back with the same report it had made an hour ago. The cops had nothing, because there was nothing. Up to a year ago he had been involved with lowlifes and illegal drugs and dirty money. He'd actually had something to worry about then and had gotten away with it, no sweat. Why sweat it now?

When pure logic, his most reliable defense, didn't provide immediate relief, he grew irritated. He didn't need the sole waitress in the place to intrude right now; but there she was, standing by his elbow.

"You want a refill?"

He held up a glass half full of red liquid.

"Does it look like I need one?"

She stared at the glass as if she saw a hard problem. He regarded her, amazed again at how incredibly moronic people were. She was thin, wearing a formless blue floral shift designed for a larger person, cinched at the waist. Her pinched face had good bones and might once have been pretty. Now it was frozen in a blank look. Blond hair stood out in tufts and her shoulders sloped dejectedly. What a loser. A stiff wind would blow her away, he thought. Another thought slipped in: she had the look of being hollowed out, of being only a body with nothing inside. The same impression his mother had given—when she was present at all.

The waitress gave a final, defeated glance at the glass and turned away.

That incident, trivial as it was, soured his mood further. He needed to concentrate, leave the insignificant, and regain control.

He scanned the room, looking for particular details, testing whether he still could do it. First, two young men picking at food, staring blankly ahead. Then a woman in her late thirties, dressed in too-tight clothes, broad across the hips with a doughy face. She found frequent reasons to leave her bar stool and walk near men who looked as if they might be available. So far, no takers. Finally the bartender, moving languidly through his work, conserving energy. A large Mongol-style moustache accentuated rather than hid his sunken cheeks. Tattoos on his forearms, from what Jason could see of them, might indicate a connection with bikers.

Out of a total of 16 people in the place, he had spotted the four who were potential junkies. If he were still in the business, he would have made a second, careful scan to look for narcs. They rarely came to places like this unless they were tracking a particular person. Still, he had always been as careful as possible, and always double-checked his initial conclusions.

He rewound mentally and replayed the scan. Then he noticed: his attention kept snapping back to the waitress. Though she was not a former customer or part of any group of users he had gotten to know, his brain had registered something familiar about her. The fact that he couldn't place her exactly gnawed at him.

Now he focused on her intently. She never smiled. She never stood completely still, instead swaying slowly from side to side. When she spoke to a customer, she moved both hands, but her right moved more than her left, often making a quick stab toward her ear and back. She wrote down orders with her left hand.

He rearranged the image of her face, erasing the beaten-down sadness but leaving an underlying solemn stillness. He made the blond hair lighter and gave it a home-cut bob. He made her younger, her right hand still moving toward her ear.

Everything he'd seen, or thought he'd seen, might be imagination or coincidence. And yet, a possibility was rearranging itself like a ghost jigsaw puzzle. If he added just a few more details ...

Why take a chance? He'd left that part of his life behind. Suppose he was right, then he'd have to decide what to do with the information. He'd be putting in jeopardy the solitary life he'd so carefully constructed for himself.

But he continued to watch the waitress, and when a particularly bright flash crossed his vision, he decided to act. It was time to put his imagination to rest.

He motioned to her. She finished delivering a beer to another table and then walked over.

"What's your name?"

She stared blankly, as if she hadn't heard, looking somewhere halfway up the wall behind him. Her right hand darted toward her ear and she uttered a low reply, with a rising inflection at the end, as if she was not sure herself.

"Lila?"

She looked right at him now.

His heart raced.

He'd found his sister.

He struggled to remain stony, admitting nothing.

"Okay, Lila. Bring me a refill."

DAY TWO

Jason waited across the street from the parking lot until Lila emerged and drove off in an old hatchback that listed left. Tailing her was no problem. Her car was the only one on the road, and there was enough moonlight that he could leave his headlights off.

From the bar's shadowed corner, he'd watched Lila for another hour, pretending total indifference when she came by to check on his drink. At closing time, he'd gone to his car.

As he drove, he hadn't yet decided why he was following her. It couldn't be something as simple as curiosity. He was curious about lots of things, but never acted solely on that instinct. His elevated heartbeat was like an itch that needed scratching. It didn't matter why: he just wanted to know more about his sister.

Her car stopped in front of a duplex at the edge of the community, and the moon's glow outlined forested hills rising behind it. She went into the unit on the left; a few minutes later a woman who seemed a little older than Lila came out, walked across the common front yard, and entered the other unit. Lights were still on in Lila's half. Jason left his car and walked to the back of the duplex where he just missed stepping in a low inflatable wading pool, but easily avoided a jungle gym.

Lila was in a dimly lit room, leaning over a bed. The window's height blocked out anything below her waist. He could see the tops of a small table, a chair, and a low cabinet with its doors closed. The room was sparse, but neat and apparently clean. It was touched with color—a red and yellow cushion on the chair, crepe ribbons and geometric pictures in florescent shades tacked to the walls. Lila straightened back up. She was holding a child, a boy.

She held the child tenderly, his head resting on her shoulder and tucked into the hollow of her neck. Lila began the same kind of swaying he'd seen earlier. Through the window glass, Jason heard her crooning a soft song, a lullaby he halfway recognized. She added a slow dance step to the cadence of the music and began a larger circle around the room, coming closer to the window. The child raised his head and opened his eyes, before closing them and lowering his head again.

His mind flashed on an image of his childhood: a photo in full color. Six children stood in a straight line, each dressed in their one set of good clothes. Lila looked peaceful, wearing a tiny smile. By her side was a younger boy—was that Nate?—with a scared look. Three others, heads hung down, stared at their shoes. At the end of the row, he saw himself with light, almost white, blond hair in a bowl cut, wide-open light blue eyes glaring defiantly at the camera. When Lila's child had raised his head, he saw the same shaped face, the white-blond hair and identical eyes, minus the defiance.

Suddenly his muscles could no longer support him. Weakness flowed from his center to his extremities, and he took a step to the side to maintain balance. He tried to keep his eyes on Lila and the boy, but they and the room were out of focus. When control returned, the light in the room had gone out and he saw only his own moonlit reflection in the window glass.

He stood there until he noticed an elongated area of light on the ground beyond a side window, and he moved toward it. Close to the house, but outside the pool of light, he looked through another window at an angle. The neat, cared-for impression he got from the child's bedroom was obliterated by the chaos of what he now observed. Lila, slumped and pale, stood at a sink filled with dirty dishes. Her arms hung listlessly at her side and her habitual body movement was stilled. Behind her, he saw smears and torn sections of wallpaper that once might have been a cream color. Visible through an opening in the wall, light from a single table lamp fell on a sofa with patches of stuffing pushing out, and on a floor strewn with pizza boxes and magazines.

Lila led a sad, disorganized, nearly hopeless existence. Yet she still made an effort to give her child a life of cleanliness and beauty. That realization was all Jason could handle until he knew what to do with the conflicting feelings smashing around inside him. He snuck back to his car and drove home slowly, constructing a plan of action.

What he decided on the drive came down to two simple conclusions. One, he needed to get out of the drug business completely. No more hanging around the perimeter, playing games. And two, he needed to get the cops off his back once and for all.

He didn't traffic in drugs anymore, but that didn't mean he was ignorant about what was going on in the drug world. Being informed was an important part of avoiding arrest. He monitored electronic and telephone conversations. He still cruised old haunts and picked up samples. Drugs never stood still; jumpy users got bored quickly and were always on the lookout for the newest and coolest trip. Recently, he'd heard talk of a new high from something called "Salvation", rumored to be way cooler and spookier than Ecstasy.

If he wanted out, he'd have to organize his information into a bargaining chip. He knew the understaffed cops were always playing catch-up in the crazy, shifting world that he followed closely. Somewhere in there was information the cops would need and he could use to get away. He needed an advantage, a bargaining chip different from others he'd possessed. Before, he used advantage to win a game.

Now he might use it to change his life.

He had reached a hill looking down on Portal. Darkness was draining away from the sky above, replaced with the start of a dawn's new light, promising good weather for the day ahead.

Maybe for him, too. But he wouldn't count on anything yet.

5:06 AM

The digital clock was still easy to read, even in a room now bright with sun. Normally Calla would have pulled on an eye shade and slept another hour, but there was no way she'd get back to sleep this time.

Lonny. Lonny. Lonny. While his presence in her life had, overall, felt like climbing a steep hill against the wind, during much of the last two years the feeling had been close to a level walk. He wasn't sleeping on the streets. He wasn't getting in trouble. He even went on plant walks with her once in a while, collecting samples with some of the youthful energy she remembered from their childhood. That's what had lulled her into thinking that maybe he could have a life something like normal. And if he did, she might hope for the same.

Yesterday's crash felt all the worse for that false hope. Huge.

Overwhelming. There were things she had to do, and she might as well use the early hours to get them done. But her body felt like a dead weight bound to the bed frame by a heavy band across her chest.

She knew she had to stop blaming herself. She'd used her knowledge of psychology to examine her sense of responsibility for Lonny, even getting some professional counseling about it. That burden, she ultimately understood, wasn't primarily psychological. Lonny was a link to her mother, to her childhood and to her heritage. The heritage that she and Lonny shared was being made inconsequential, often obliterated, by a bigger, dominant culture. The threat to their heritage was real, and the instinct to preserve was natural. In helping Lonny, she did much more: she preserved in herself the good aspects of her childhood, and she preserved parts of her heritage that should—that needed to—survive.

She knew all along that looking after Lonny had to go hand in hand with her persistent effort to succeed in a career. She'd managed to finish high school, put together two part-time jobs at law firms in Esterhill, then gradually gathered enough credits over six and a half years to earn a degree at the local campus and eventually an M.A. in social work. She did all that on her own, leaning on others as little as possible.

The only trouble was that she did a better job of taking care of Lonny than of taking care of herself. Lonny had an unconscious but effective mode of surviving, if he could be kept away from bad influences. He'd become something like a community mascot, basically sweet. People gave him things: clothes, tools. Someone must have given him or loaned him the pickup he was sleeping in near the place where they found Rolf's body.

But where did Lonny get that truck? Normally he got around on a light motorcycle. During the snow season, he bummed rides or hitched a lot. She could imagine someone loaning him a truck, but why on that particular night? She needed to find out.

She could see the shape of the day ahead: first a call to her boss to see how her most urgent cases could be handed off until she could return full-time. Then she would call Sonia. But all that was at least two hours away.

She was still in bed. Concentrating on what to do had already had one good effect: she no longer felt that heavy band across her chest, clamping her down. She knew she could face the day. She'd tidy the place, shower, have breakfast and be fully ready. Tired, yes, but focused. Then, call her boss. Next, call Sonia.

And find out how Lonny got his truck.

6:05 AM

Greg's mother had his breakfast waiting. By unspoken mutual agreement they had chosen these weekly early morning meetings, after other times of the day had turned out to be unpredictable.

She was leaning against the stove, arms folded, wearing a plain housedress with Ukrainian stitching that she had added around the hem and sleeves. In sturdy shoes, she was a stolid and watchful presence, her gray hair announcing middle age. She rose so early that she was always up when he arrived, regardless of the hour. He had no idea when and what she ate, but his food was always ready. And always the same: hot rolled oats, rye bread and plain yoghurt, the closest his mother could come to *kasha* and *kefir*, the traditional Ukrainian breakfast fare.

Finished, he thanked his mother—sincerely, but in the outwardly emotionless way that was so much a part of the culture they had brought with them to America. Underneath was a fierce family bond, never fully revealed to outsiders.

He took his police notebook and a cup of coffee out to the back yard and sat at the replica of the US Park Service table his father had built. The sun was already high enough that its slanting light escaped the mountain ridge and the tall Ponderosas, falling on half of their back yard. His perch was still in shadow, though, making it easier for him to read through the most recent email on his smartphone.

The last two messages, stamped just five minutes ago, caught his attention. One informed him that the lab tox report on Rolf was complete. He could read the results by logging in to the department's secure web site. The other was from Chief Cisek, saying that he wanted to see Greg at 8:00 am. He'd look at the tox results after checking his other email, looking for a message from one sender in particular.

Olga emailed almost every day, often more than once. Today's message, titled "Important/OK?" made Greg's heart leap. It was definite: a week from now Olga, along with two other translators, would fly to New York for a four-day course at the United Nations headquarters on international resources for nation-building. She could stay another three days over a long weekend before she had to return to Egypt. On that weekend she would be able to fly to Seattle so that she and Greg could spend at least two days together.

Her final sentence left him an out.

"I will make no travel arrangements from New York until you tell me to."

Maybe she wondered how much he really wanted to see her. Greg's heart was in charge when he wrote a reply in Russian.

"I count the days to be with you again and hold you near. Please send information on your arrival, my dear one.

In Russian, he was more emotional that he would have been in the terser English he used every day. Regardless of the language, he meant every word. Yet his finger paused over the "Send" button as his brain clicked into a different rhythm. That's really nice and you really do want to see her. But have you *actually* thought of how difficult it may be to spend time with her in the middle of an investigation? How are you going to manage the time off? The Rolf case could turn out to be an accident; or it might be a homicide, accidental or deliberate. Either way, he could not imagine that the workload, and the need for single-minded attention to it, would diminish much before Olga arrived. Olga could rent a car and drive herself over the pass if necessary. But how would she interpret his failure to be at the airport?

He put everything else out of his mind to concentrate fully on Olga. Details like an airport pickup didn't matter that much. What he was wrestling with lay deeper. He said he was glad she took the Cairo job. But was he really? During their travels together, thoughts about the two of them sharing a life—a home, possibly children—had been constant. But doubt started to nag him when he returned alone to the Cascades. Did she feel the same way, or had she already changed in her love for him? Was it possible she was making the trip to Seattle just to be able to tell him face to face that she no longer could see him in her future?

Stop! Stop! He'd need to deal with those questions, but not now. He still had a few days to figure things out. Right now he had to concentrate. He reread the message and punched "Cancel".

Back to work. He needed either to clear Jason Ferris or to help Espy and McHugh dig deeper into Ferris' alibi. The tech people might find that information on the thumb drive showed Ferris couldn't have left his home the night of Rolf's death. But would that be real proof? If Ferris was as devious as McHugh said, then maybe the data had been doctored. Or someone else could have been at Ferris' house while he poisoned Rolf. He could almost hear McHugh's voice, laced with anger and frustration, arguing for that interpretation, even if their tech people said the data cleared his favorite suspect.

Maybe he should listen more closely to McHugh. After all, McHugh knew Ferris, had a long history with him. On the other hand, listening didn't need to include unquestioning acceptance of his judgment.

A comment by one of his instructors at the Police Academy had made a big impression on him: that both facts and instincts could be liabilities in investigations if you relied only on one to the exclusion of the other. So he tried to look at what both of them told him in the case of Ferris.

Factually, he had little to work with. It was a fact that, instead of fleeing, Ferris had stayed home and had been willing to talk. He didn't show any of the disoriented, furtive behaviors that were sometimes a tip-off for guilt. But maybe he was just good at covering up.

Instinctively, he was on his guard about Ferris. Regardless of what McHugh thought about guilt or innocence, he was on the money about Ferris' intelligence. Apart from that, Greg had the intuitive sense that Ferris was more of a planner than a plunger, that he coldly calculated odds, and that he acted personally only after exhausting possibilities for getting others to do his bidding. Ferris might be devious, but he wasn't impulsive or careless. He was probably an excellent gamer.

Another feeling that he had about Ferris was weaker, but still might be significant: Ferris was lonely. Despite always being with his family and having a protective older sister, Greg had known loneliness growing up—loneliness that he had come to understand as part of being an outsider: a Ukrainian among Russians, a Pentecostal among the Orthodox, an immigrant among people with roots. Being in the same room with Ferris had given him an unexpected feeling of kinship. Ferris seemed at least as much outsider as outlaw.

Factually, Ferris might be *a* good suspect. But Greg was not ready to buy the idea that he was the only person earning scrutiny. Harland Casey came across as helpful, but was he just putting on a solicitous act, using volubility as cover? There was nothing factual to tie Casey to the investigation; instinct, however, warned that Casey might not be telling everything he knew.

Finally, there was Gabby Thibodeau. Maybe he shouldn't be on the list. But he probably knew something of value. He claimed that he had met Lonny only on a couple of occasions, yet that seemed unlikely. Lonny slept often at the hatchery and Gabby was the night watchman; they had to cross path more than occasionally. Either Gabby considered random contact unimportant, or was hiding something. Either way, Greg wanted to talk to Gabby again.

The yard was now fully covered with sunlight. He savored its warmth for a few minutes. This was a perfect temperature, during what he thought of as the best hours of the best days of the year. There were never too many of them. Later in the summer, these early mornings would be hot, and then they would change all too suddenly to the chill of early fall.

8:26 AM

"We've got enough to charge Lonny Ogden. The case is still being made, so I can't tell you the exact charge yet. But the time's come to hold him on a charge instead of stringing out his status as a person of interest. His lawyer's been pushing us on that."

That off his ample chest, Chief Cisek creaked back in his chair to gauge Phil's reaction.

That was terrible news. It would crush Calla, but Phil wasn't about to reveal his conflicted emotions and their source, even to a friend like Tom Cisek. He scanned the chief's face, looking for reactions that would tell him more than the straight facts he'd just heard.

"Thanks, Tom, I appreciate your keeping me in the loop. Does Ogden's sister know?"

Cisek's poker face didn't change.

"The lawyer will tell her as soon as the charge is made."

Phil's mind could not let go of Calla and how she would react to the news. Without really thinking about it, he let out a question, an old reporter's trick to keep a conversation going until something relevant arose.

"Anything else I should know?"

"What about?"

He tried to sound more definite than he felt.

"C'mon, Tom. You know what I have in mind—your usual tips on how individuals in the department are doing on the case. You know as well as I do that it's often the information that individuals have given out unintentionally that has caused us our biggest PR problems. It makes my job easier to know what's been leaked, accidentally or otherwise, and if there's unusual friction in your shop."

Cisek sat still for a moment. The chair creaked again as he leaned forward and clasped his meaty hands on top of the desk.

"Bill McHugh. Not one of my guys, but he's on the case."

"I know him."

"'Course you do, and you've requested him a lot for school visits and city celebrations."

"He's well known from the time he spends up here at the sheriff's substation. People like him. Might as well get some mileage out of that. Besides, he shows up on time, and he's courteous and appropriate."

"That's his good side, all right. On the job he can also be bullheaded, and too aggressive."

"People have different styles. I don't get the drift of what we're talking about."

Cisek nodded.

"Him and Takarchuk."

Phil visualized the puzzlement he must be showing. Cisek smiled.

"Don't know what you're thinking, Phil, but it's likely wrong. All I got is this. Espy told me he sees tension building between Takarchuk and McHugh. Without telling you more than I should, Takarchuk's open-minded about things that McHugh has already made up his mind on."

Phil thought about that.

"Okay, that's good to know, but I'm not sure why you want me to know it. I'm guessing you think Greg might come to me for advice, and I might say something that could make his relations with McHugh worse. If that's what you mean, I get it. But I haven't crossed that line and don't intend to."

Cisek eyed him; during the town's last murder case Phil had to admit he almost did cross an important line. The unblinking stare on Cisek's face was waiting for more from him than weak intent.

"I hear you loud and clear."

"Hope so."

"We're copasetic?"

There might as well have been a "harumph" in front of the chief's parting words.

"For now. Just mind your shop and let me mind mine. I'll pass on what I think you need to know."

Phil didn't need that reminder, hardly heard it. Calla and what she was about to hear drowned out everything else.

9:10 AM

Calla stood by her car after an early visit to a client and let her mind roam over the large field of new timothy hay that spread out before her, as if the field hid answers. At moments like this, nature usually calmed her with a sense of the vast interconnectedness of the world, pushing immediate worries away. But that calm refused to appear.

She turned on her silenced cell phone and got an unexpected lift: Phil Bianchi had called. She was halfway through dialing a reply, when her phone signaled an incoming call. A glance at her screen told her it wasn't Phil trying again, but her lawyer Sonia. She punched on, and must have been distracted by thoughts of Phil, because she had to ask Sonia to repeat what she said. The irritation level rose in Sonia's voice.

"I said that you'd have to talk to Lonny. He's being cagey and weird, refusing to talk to me. It's like he doesn't understand how much trouble he's in. I don't have time to deal with that hassle. I warned you that his willingness to have me as his counsel could change."

Calla tried to conjure up an image of Lonny twenty miles away.

"I don't know what to say, Sonia. He ought to be able to see that his situation is serious."

"You'd think. But that's not the case. Trust me or don't trust me when I tell you that. I don't care. *You've* got to talk to him. *You've* got to convince him to tell what happened. Depending on what he says, we might be able to get him released. Otherwise, he'll stay where he is … Hold on."

Sonia swore under her breath.

"I've got to take another call. One second."

Silence descended on Calla. She held the phone to her ear and tried to think, but thinking felt like letting more air out of a tire that was already severely deflated. She had clients who depended on her, and she'd be of no use to them if Lonny stayed in jail. He needed Sonia, and she couldn't move forward without Sonia's help. How could she get through to him? Their first encounter in his jail cell had not been encouraging. Maybe a direct approach was not the way in. A thought occurred. At first she was dubious, then intrigued. Maybe the old stories could reach him.

Their mother had found part of her strength in tribal legends, which she passed on to her children. In Native American lore, the legends dealt with daily life and with the great mysteries in nature that created and sustained life. Life wasn't boiled down to theories, conditions, and syndromes as it was in her psych books. Her mother's explanations were woven into stories that sprang from a great knowable and unknowable whole. You couldn't grasp the explanations without surrendering to the stories, like the one about *Enum-Klah*, the Thunderbird, and about how Eagle took away Skunk's power.

The trip on which the story took you was as valuable as its conclusion. Everything was connected and ongoing: the heroes and the villains, animals and humans, the mystical and the real, all enveloped in nature. Nature, the rewarder and the punisher.

Until her mother began the last part of her long, sad slide downward, she told those stories. Drunk or high, her slurred voice clung to them. When she passed into incoherence, Calla would continue them, partly for herself, partly for Lonny. From the time he was a toddler, he responded to them, fascinated.

Lonny, sitting cross-legged on the floor listening to the old stories, was the only image Calla had of him being still. His constant twitches were gone, and the need to rearrange parts of his body every few seconds disappeared. A blissful smile glowed when the story told of happiness and success; fear rimmed his eyes during descriptions of revenge and punishment.

Sonia clicked back onto the line. She heard the rising tension in Sonia's voice before she registered the words.

"Calla, you're not going to like this. The body they found was poisoned. The DA's office has opened an official murder investigation. Lacking any other leads, guess who their prime suspect is? You need to go now."

10:07 AM

Greg parked in the small lot at the edge of Pioneer Park. The playground was empty this time of morning. A single jogger stretched her hamstrings under the high firs at the far corner of the green square of lawn.

He'd stopped here to review what he'd learned at the morning's briefing but, switching off the ignition, his thoughts shifted instead to the time, months ago, when he met Olga, and to the moment when friendship shifted into intimacy at this spot. Here she was again, right here with him, all the desire he had for her, all the indecision he had about where their relationship was going. Her strong sense of presence was an inescapable reminder that he had to resolve the question of her visit. He could no longer put it off.

Since Olga had arrived in Cairo, his mind had adopted a dual time mode: what he was doing in Central Washington, and what Olga was doing nine hours ahead of him, close to where the Mediterranean Sea met the Suez Canal. It was early evening for her now, though she was probably still in her office. On his cell he pushed a familiar speed dial.

Olga answered immediately. Her voice had an impatient edge.

"Glad you called. Are you ready to talk about whether you want me to come to Swiftwater?"

"Are you all right?"

"Sorry to sound rushed. I'm translating a crucial meeting in a few minutes. I can't talk long. How about you? Are you all right and have you thought about my visit?"

"I'm fine, and I want you to come."

There was a long pause.

"I can't make out whether you sound distracted or maybe not enthusiastic. Or it's just that I'm rushed. Maybe we need to talk later. But if I'm to make reservations, it can't wait much longer. Call me tomorrow. Sorry, I really have to go."

With that, her voice was gone. For five minutes, Greg found various ways of kicking himself—for not being sure about what he wanted to say, for revealing his indecision, for planting doubt, for calling at all. At least he knew that he had the ball now. The next time he phoned Olga, he had to be sure he believed his own words before asking her to believe them.

He wrenched his mind back to the latest information: they had found a partial fingerprint on the Swizzler wrapper at the crime scene. Preliminary analysis did not rule out the possibility that it could be Lonny's. Lonny insisted that he had not been at the service station that night, but when shown a picture of Lonny, the attendant at the service station said Lonny had been there some time recently; he just couldn't swear it had been on the night in question. In any case, the station had closed at 9:00 pm, and the coroner established a time of death between 11:30 pm and 12:30 am.

The tox report showed that the cookie that Rolf had eaten was laced with a poison that might have come from a native plant like wolfbane or white snake root. But those plant materials were only part of a complex cocktail of drugs. One was crystal meth, the home-cooked scourge of the county. Of every county in the state, really. The second ingredient was salvia, a simple sage plant that, like its cousin peyote, could produce a low-level, short-lived hallucinatory high. Salvia could be grown just about anywhere and wasn't illegal in most states, including Washington. The salvia in the victims' cookies had been chemically bonded to DMT, officially dimethyltryptamine, another naturally-occurring hallucinogen.

There was, however, one more drug in the mix that no one could pinpoint. According to the Federal DEA data base, the same concoction had appeared before in limited quantities, mostly in southwestern states. It had shown up in Washington only two years ago, Greg learned.

So far, the police in Kittinach County had been calling the new drug just that, "the new drug". A few were also beginning to refer to it by the name used in the shadow world of drug users: "Salvation". It would probably have other names by now; meth had more than fifteen street names.

But unlike meth, the garage band of drugs, Salvation hadn't spread rapidly. It was too sophisticated. The DEA was at a loss about where it came from.

When the meeting had broken up, Greg took a closer look at the tox report. The autopsy had more specifically noted that the fatal cookie was chocolate chip. Harland Casey had said that Lonny liked chocolate chip cookies.

Greg would eventually report that fact to Espy and McHugh, but that alone was not exactly evidence. So maybe he ought to interview Casey again, and see if the man had anything further to add. He put the car in gear and drove the short distance to the hatchery.

Greg found Casey and his wife Janice washing windows inside the visitors' center building. Janice worked at floor level while Casey towered over her from the lower rungs of a stepladder. Casey saw him come in and rapidly descended the ladder.

"Hi there Mr. Policemen Greg you're out bright and early and so are we Janice here said she was sick and tired of these dirty windows and since this place only gets one washing a year and only outside because of budget cutbacks we decided to have a go at the inside with Janice doing what she can reach and me doing the rest from up on the ladder ..."

There was no telling how long Casey might go on. Greg cut in as politely as possible.

"Good morning. Sorry to interrupt; but I wonder, Mrs. Casey, if I could borrow your husband for a few minutes? It shouldn't take long."

Janice Casey dropped a cloth into the bucket at her feet and shifted her weight to her arm crutch. She wiped her right hand on a floral apron and looked up at where she had been working, then across the expanse of remaining unwashed windows. The weariness etched into her forehead found its way into her voice.

"I suppose, if you have to. I'll just keep pecking away, see how much I can do on my own."

She aimed the last phrase at her husband. He didn't miss its message.

"Janice is a trooper, isn't she, what with her infirmity and all but you can't keep her down I'll need to get back soon..."

"I don't have much to ask. I just want to see again where Lonny slept, and check on a couple of things."

Casey took longer than he needed to in moving his ladder and fussing with his window washing gear. Reluctance slowed him, and it showed.

Janice's voice took on a sharper edge in her parting comment.

"Go on Harland. But don't you dawdle. Get back here soon so we can finish."

Casey nodded dutifully before leading Greg to the main hatchery area. The vehicle gate was down and the sliding gate in the chain link fence stood open. Casey strode on, his word torrent temporarily dammed up.

In the rear storage building, they threaded through equipment to Lonny's cramped sleeping area. Greg saw signs that the forensic tech had been there: the blanket was in a different position and, when looked up at the shelf for the cardboard box that had the packages of Swizzlers, it was gone.

He gave the small room a quick search before addressing Casey.

"You mentioned before that Lonny liked licorice Swizzlers, and we found two packages. You also said he especially liked chocolate chip cookies, but there's no sign of them around here."

Casey's eyes wandered the cramped space. When his attention returned, there was a different tone in his voice and a sly look flashed across his eyes, followed by something that may have been relief.

"You probably ought to talk to Janice about that."

"And why is that?"

"Well, she does the baking and all and knows what Lonny likes."

They found Janice half seated, half sprawled on one of the upholstered chairs in the entryway of the visitors' center. She rose part way, then sank back down wearing a look that mixed distress and apology.

"Sometimes I just get tired. It got hard to go on alone. But I'm about ready to get back at it."

It never hurt to be courteous.

"Can I get you a glass of water?"

"I appreciate your offer, young man ..."

She sent a tight smile her husband's way, raising her index finger like a schoolmarm.

"You could have come back a little sooner, Harland. You know I don't do well without you. And yes, I could use a glass of water. Why don't you get it? It's your penance."

Casey played his part, hanging his head in imitation sheepishness as he went off toward the rear of the building. Greg wondered: was this the way they always interacted? Or was it for his benefit? Having the two of them together complicated communication. He was glad to have Janice to himself.

"I understand you make good chocolate chip cookies."

She looked surprised by the abrupt change of subject.

"Some people would say so."

"Would those people include Lonny?"

This time her smile included genuine warmth.

"Poor lost Lonny. Yes, he likes my cookies and sometimes, I like to think, he gets a feeling of comfort and safety when he eats them."

The smile faded, replaced by worry.

"I hear from Harland that Lonny's in trouble. Here's hoping it's all just a big mistake. The kid has had a hard life and he doesn't need it to get worse. Is he all right?"

He stuck to procedure.

"Lonny is currently being questioned by the police in connection with the recent murder. You've probably heard about it."

"I have, but I can't imagine how Lonny could have been involved."

He heard Casey returning and hurried his next comment.

"We're just investigating at this point. While I'm here, I don't suppose you have any of your famous cookies so I could have a taste?"

Janice looked at him quizzically.

"I'm all out. I can bake you some new ones, but I think you want those cookies for more than their taste. If you think my husband is involved with Lonny's problems, just say so. Otherwise, leave us alone."

He kicked himself. He could have been less obvious. Harland arrived, his practiced joviality back in place. He made an ostentatious bow.

"Your water, madame, cool and refreshing, just as requested."

Janice took a sip and Greg offered words that he hoped would reassure her. He might still need her cooperation later on.

"Thanks for your time. I still look forward to tasting your cookies."

As he left, Casey beamed and Janice's wary eyes followed him over the rim of her glass.

10:14 AM

The same officer as before unlocked the holding cell. Calla watched Lonny pace, turn, pace again, look at her, sit on the steel cot attached to the wall, and begin constant fidgeting. His black hair was a tangled bird's nest and his dark skin couldn't hide the pallor of exhaustion. He didn't rise to greet her. In fact, he wouldn't look at her. She remained standing.

"Good morning, Lonny. You all right?"

Silence.

"I don't imagine you got much sleep."

Still no reply. Lonny at his most obstinate. What else should she have expected?

"Okay, I get it. You're mad. I don't know why, but I can't let that get in the way of helping you."

His only reaction was more nervous movement.

"I don't know whether you really understand how serious your situation is. But you could go to jail for a long time if the police think you were at that place where the man was killed night before last. Did you go there?"

This time she got a furtive look, then a whispered reply she had to lean forward to hear.

"Don't know. I was tired. Maybe."

Calla reached toward him without touching.

"Sonia is your best hope. You need to be honest with her. Help her so she can help you. She'll be here to talk to you again in about an hour."

Now she got a defiant glare that lasted. Calla leaned against the cold concrete wall of the cell and closed her eyes. Through the haze of her own fear, she tried to summon calmness. She tried to summon their mother's musical voice.

"You remember the story of the dead salmon and Old Man Rattlesnake?"

His face softened slightly, but his voice was still a whisper.

"People didn't obey the Creator about caring for the salmon, and all the salmon stopped coming up the river."

Her cadence imitated the ripple of a gentle stream. Lonny didn't move from the bed, but he hoisted up his legs and crossed them, putting his hands on his knees. His expression recalled the rapt little boy who once sat by her feet.

"The people found one dead salmon by the river and asked Old Man Rattlesnake to help make him alive again, and after a while the old man said yes. But he moved too slow, and Coyote got to the fish first and moved it with a stick, and tried to fool the people into thinking the salmon was alive when it wasn't."

Lonny spoke up.

"And Old Man Rattlesnake jumped across the salmon four times and something magic happened. The fifth time Old Man Rattlesnake disappeared into the fish and the fish jumped into the river and all the fish returned."

He repeated that part of the story almost exactly the way their mother would have told it.

"That's right, Lonny, and the people were happy, weren't they, when the salmon came back?"

A vigorous nod and a smile.

"Do you remember what mama said when she finished the story?"

Lonny's expression dropped to puzzlement. She prompted him.

"She said that you don't want to be a dead salmon, isn't that right?"

The question got a careful nod in return. She gave him a chance to say more, and when he didn't, she went on.

"I think mama was trying to tell both of us that bad people can hurt us. Hurt us badly, if we let them, and then we're like the dead salmon. But even if we get hurt, we can get help. The salmon got help from Old Rattlesnake. You can get help if you want it."

Something got through. His eyes clung to hers and she thought she read a glint of interest in them. She took a chance.

"The salmon might have liked Old Rattlesnake, but maybe not. You don't have to like Sonia for her to help you. All you have to do is let her help. Just like the salmon and Old Rattlesnake."

For a moment, she thought that her gamble was a loss. Lonny's eyes dropped. He moved one leg over the edge of the steel cot and started fidgeting again. But, to her surprise, the leg stilled, and his gaze returned to her face.

"Okay. She can come."

Her mood rose: Lonny's inner door was open a crack. Why not look for one other possibility the story had raised as she told it? She offered an encouraging smile.

"That's good, Lonny! That's good! I'll call Sonia and let her know. And while she's here, you might want to talk to her about something else."

His quizzical expression mixed with faint suspicion, but she decided to go on.

"You remember the Stick-showers, who they are?"

Stick-showers—*Ste-ye-hah'*—mysterious, huge, nocturnal people, devious and rarely seen. If you become crazed, suffer an accident, lose your way and hear mysterious noises, the Stick-showers are at work.

Lonny swallowed hard.

"They hurt you. They're bad news. Don't trust 'em."

"That's right. You might want to tell Sonia if there are any Stick-showers in your life."

His reaction was instantaneous. Both legs shoved out over the edge of the cot. His head swiveled off to one side toward the wall and his body listed, taken over by a continuous tremor.

She waited anxiously. Suddenly, he flung his body back around so he could stare at her, eyes wide and terrified.

"Don't like the Stick-showers. Don't like 'em. Don't talk about them, Calla."

He twisted back to the wall and descended into silence. He was still silent five minutes later when the guard returned, opening the door and motioning for her to exit the cell.

She tried one last time.

"Please just talk to Sonia, Lonny. She can help you, like Old Man Rattlesnake."

Lonny turned his head slightly and nodded without making eye contact. The door closed with a clang, a cruel, weighty sound that joined the other disturbances in her heart.

10:30 AM

Jason was finished with his computer traffic. He read lots of messages on the murder, many concluding that police investigations might spill over into a crackdown on drug users. None of the message writers had any idea that Jason was listening in. Yes, he was getting out of the drug business, but by no means could he afford to lose track of it. Especially not now.

When he had been active, he learned fast how unreliable the drug world was. The best protection was to have better information than anyone else. Most of all, to have better—and better protected—information than the police. Police in rural areas were understaffed, especially when it came to computer experts. He had all the time in the world, and state-of-the-art equipment, besides.

Druggies and their suppliers were a mixed lot; but just like everyone else, they needed communication. They knew that the DEA and local narcs did their best to monitor email and cellphone traffic; the druggies welcomed any opportunity to talk to each other securely.

He became their most important asset toward that goal. He offered an informal service: any time he paid a visit, he would throw in, free of charge, a computer security check. If he found breaches, he promised to eliminate them. His clients accepted his offer in droves.

What they didn't know was that during his visits Jason also installed spy software of his own design, enabling him to monitor from his house any computer on which he had run a check. He received daily reports of the keystrokes on the users' computers, which might be more secure against the electronic eye of the law, but were decidedly more accessible to him. After he stopped actively distributing drugs, he still dropped in on old suppliers and users and introduced himself to new ones. His previous offer of free computer checks was never withdrawn, and his network remained robust. When he spent his morning hours in front of the screens and the data rolled by, he was greeting his herd of Trojan horses, trotting in dutifully to unload the information they'd picked up during the night.

That took care of email and instant messages. As his former clients changed their communication mode from desktop computers to smartphones, Jason added an offer to check the security of phones as well as computers. Soon he had created another network of cloned SIM cards and phone numbers that reported conversations around the network directly to his phone.

But this morning a new thought intruded on Jason's usual satisfaction with what he'd created. Yes, the information was protection; but in the bright spotlight of the murder investigation, it could also mean increased exposure if it were detected by the police.

He wasn't ready yet to shut down his data-gathering completely. He could still think of uses for it. But was it time to set up a foolproof way of destroying his old hard drives? Or should he remove his backup storage devices from the safe in the wall of his basement? There was nothing on them that would incriminate him directly, but he could imagine a clever lawyer using his possession of the data to convince a willing jury that he was in fact a drug kingpin. That, he didn't need.

Wait! He was getting immersed too soon in future details. That wasn't like him. He knew, but was hesitant to admit, the cause for the unsteady reasoning that had lately disturbed his orderly thinking: Lila and the boy. Had his encounter with them made him more cautious about a lifestyle that he had thought of as impregnable? No, that was too big a question. Break it down. It was his rediscovered relatives themselves that were the problem. It was they, not his thoughts about them, that created confusion.

Lila had been walled off with the rest of his past for so long that it should be easy to put her back behind the wall. Some trivial memory must have been blown out of proportion last night. The strange flashes across his eyes could have a completely separate explanation. They were no more than glitches, things he could fix with a simple rewrite or a patch. Reality always trumps imagination. Once he rearranged things that way, it was logical to pay Lila another visit. See her for what she really was in broad daylight. Then his brain would clear.

He made his usual detailed check of the house, set the alarms, and pulled his Chevy out of the garage. The two-year-old sedan was a tan color, plain and anonymous; Jason passed models exactly like his car all around the county. Everything else was hidden: the heavy shocks, supercharger, milled heads and high-end radials. He'd never tested the car at more than eighty-five on a quiet back road, much less taken it to its limit. Like much of what he owned, the car's special capabilities were a contingency, an insurance policy covering extreme emergency.

On the way to Lila's house he drove just under the speed limit. Two cowboys in their pickup passed him on a curve and flicked him the finger. He couldn't have cared less.

He parked on a widening of the road a few hundred yards from Lila's duplex. The last part he walked though firs and Ponderosas where the underbrush and grasses were already well dried out. He was some distance away when he spotted Lila and the boy in her back yard.

She sat in an aluminum folding chair that didn't have much life left in it, in the middle of play equipment around her that had faded to a dull reminder of its original colors. The boy was picking up toys and throwing them into the wading pool. When he'd found all the toys, he stepped into the shallow water and made a pantomime fuss about how cold it was, adding playful shrieks for emphasis. Then, satisfied that he had his mother's attention, he threw the toys back out onto the lawn, and took a few turns down the low slide before starting the cycle over again.

Jason hadn't been aware that he'd moved closer to get a better view. He thought the cover of the underbrush would make him invisible, and was utterly unprepared when Lila spoke in his direction.

"Why don't you come out, Jason?"

He stood stock still.

Lila spoke again.

"I recognized you last night in the bar."

He still didn't move, but words formed of their own accord.

"Why didn't you say so?"

She looked down at the ground as if she might find her answer there.

"I was ashamed that you saw me. Saw what I've become. I didn't think you'd want anything to do with me."

He was trying to think of what to say when she spoke again.

"Do you want a cup of coffee?"

His voice answered for him.

"Okay."

She rose and called to the boy.

"C'mon, Jace, let's go inside."

Lila wore a faint smile. It was as if she had read his reeling mind.

"Yes, I named him for you."

For a moment, Jason's balance gave way and he couldn't tell whether he was rising or falling.

10:45 PM

Where did Lonny get that truck? Following the only guess she could come up with, Calla found the small farm outside Thermal on her second try. It was on 408 Road, a designation that corresponded to a grid sighted out by some long-gone Corps of Engineers surveyor more than a century ago. GPS might help you to your destination on a rural road like this one, but she still used her most tried and true method: ask the locals.

She knew about the Haynes farm, though this would be her first visit. Actually, what she knew was the reputation of the Haynes family. Most families had members with similar traits and behaviors. If a couple of kids performed well in school or work, and didn't hang out with the wrong people or do drugs, chances were decent that all the family members would be like that.

This wasn't the case for the Haynes. Both parents worked, Al Haynes on the farm and Patricia at a local bank. Three girls were straight arrows, one an honor student. But the other four Haynes children—the three brothers, born close together, and the youngest of the four girls—were trouble from early on. The parents didn't seem to care; they kept up a public pretense of being normal, upstanding folks, nurtured their good kids and ignored the bad ones.

Terry, the middle boy, came to Calla's attention because he and Lonny had met at a school "game day". Lonny hated any situation where he might end up being tagged a loser, so he drifted to a corner of the park and sat cross-legged, staring away from the raucous whirlwind around him. She had watched a wiry kid join Lonny and squat next to him most of the day. They'd stayed together, off and on, since then, and increasingly after Terry began cruising the county in an old beater he'd fixed up. It wasn't long before the beater was replaced with a flashy, faster car. Calla suspected that Terry had introduced Lonny to drugs.

Twice she'd met Terry in her social services capacity, both times because he was peripherally involved with someone who was in deeper trouble. As far as she knew, Terry had never been arrested, though he had been investigated several times.

After speaking to Patricia at the house, she walked around to the rear where she found a neat white-fenced horse enclosure and a huge shed stacked with bales of timothy hay. The field beyond was a gauze of green, the small shoots of a new crop on the way. Terry knelt by a big tractor in the shadow of the shed, an open box of tools beside him. When she called his name, he put aside the part he was working on and stood to meet her. His hair was clipped close to his skull, accentuating pale, freckled skin stretched taut across wide cheek bones. Though his eyes darted nervously, she saw that his hands were steady.

"Hi, Terry. I need your help. Lonny is being investigated for a murder he didn't commit. The truck he was in could be important, and I thought you might be able to tell me how he got it."

She tried to keep her voice friendly, though any residual friendship from Terry's childhood encounters with Lonny had long since evaporated.

Terry picked up a rag and wiped his hands.

"Didn't know he had a truck. Helped him keep his bike runnin', that's about it."

No greeting. His tone pointed out land mines in the space between them.

"Lonny doesn't have the money for a Ford 150, even a used one. I thought maybe you might have loaned it to him."

Suspicion.

"Why me?"

"You're still friends, aren't you?"

"Yeah, but I ain't got no truck like that. Sell it if I had it."

"Okay. Do you know anyone else who might have loaned him a truck?"

His eyes flicked up to hers, and stayed a little longer. He dropped the rag and picked up the part again. While still leaning over he muttered something.

"What did you say?"

Again, barely louder.

"Try up at the hatchery."

"The hatchery up at Swiftwater? Talk to who?"

She heard finality in the words that drifted over Terry's shoulder as he turned away and knelt by the tractor.

"Ain't sayin' no more."

She stared at Terry's back, wondering whether it belonged to someone who now was working against Lonny. But no anger accompanied that thought. She remembered the little boy who stayed by Lonny when other kids shunned him. Trouble just finds some people, she knew from sad experience, when they haven't found it first.

"Good luck, Terry."

She meant that, even if she had little hope that her words would make any difference.

11:56 AM

At the police station, Calla had to wait half an hour before she was allowed access to her brother. She checked her phone and saw Phil had called again. But she was crammed into a seat between two other visitors. With her shoulders right up against theirs, a private conversation would have to wait. She leafed through a magazine and must have dozed, because she had to remind herself where she was when an officer nudged her and said she could go in.

Lonny had gone back to fidgeting and looking everywhere except at her. The officer watched them from the hallway, so Calla lowered her voice to a whisper.

She told Lonny about seeing Terry, keeping the circumstances vague and mentioning a "hello" from Terry that he'd not offered. Lonny showed indifference to everything. She took a deep breath and shifted the conversation.

"I'm heading up to the hatchery, Lonny. Any message for anyone there?"

No response.

"The truck you were in is safe. But just in case it was someone at the hatchery who loaned it to you, shouldn't I let them know?"

That got a quick, alarmed glance. She pushed into the opening.

"If I owned a truck that I'd loaned to someone who got arrested and I heard about that on TV, I'd want to know what happened to my truck. Wouldn't you, Lonny?"

His movements were bigger now, feet out and back again, down on an elbow then bolt upright. She could see his jaw working.

"Maybe I should go straight to the hatchery director. He'd know what to do."

Fear was in Lonny's raised voice.

"No! No! Not him."

She glanced at the officer outside the cell, and saw him take a step forward. She lifted a hand toward him and replied to Lonny in a soothing whisper.

"Why not?"

Lonny got his voice back down.

"He don't know nothin'."

"Nothing about what?"

Sullen silence. She put her hands on her temples, trying to massage down a sudden headache.

"Lonny, we're talking about how you got your truck and you know it. What's so hard about that question?"

His agitation increased. She backed off, trying a different tack.

"I won't go to the hatchery director, but I'm still going to ask around to see if someone else can help me. Don't you want to give me a hint where to start?"

Lonny found the will to be still for a few seconds, and muttered something into his arm—a name she vaguely remembered having heard around the reservation.

"Gabby Thibodeau."

Was this one of Lonny's Stick-showers? She knew not to mention the evil spirits a second time.

"Who's he?"

"The night watchman. Works six to six."

"And he would know?"

"It's his truck."

Lonny tucked his legs up onto the bed and draped one arm over his eyes. She knew the signal. She leaned over the cot and whispered what she hoped he would hear as a loving goodbye.

Leaving the police station, Calla checked her watch and was

surprised to see it was 1:15. No wonder she was so hungry. The Sunrise Café was just up the street, as good a place as any for a quick lunch.

The comfortable front room of the Sunrise, with framed pictures of Swiftwater's past on its wood-paneled walls and a big stone fireplace unlit during the summer months, was emptying of its mid-day lunch crowd as she arrived. She was looking for a small table when she saw Phil Bianchi waving at her from a corner booth. He was already standing, wearing a tan sports coat over an open-necked shirt. She saw the empty lunch dishes.

"Hello, Phil. Finished, I see."

He smiled and extended a hand. It felt warm.

"But I haven't had my coffee yet. Sit down and we'll get Julie to take your order."

Phil sat and slid to the center of the booth, motioning for her to do the same. Once she sat down, she felt a little of her tiredness drain away and realized that his kind of company was what she needed right now. His kind? Or him? She'd had to depend on her own strength and instincts for so long that she didn't even know how to use someone else's help. Was that what she had a chance to do now?

"Thanks, Phil, And thanks, too for your calls. Sorry I couldn't reply right away. Lonny's been charged with murder. That took precedence over everything else."

Concern was etched on his face. His hand moved in her direction, then back.

"Chief Cisek tipped me off this morning that that was likely to happen. I tried to call you."

She managed a nod. At least she was spared the effort of a lengthier explanation.

They sat in silence, his eyes not leaving her face, until he spoke again.

"How is Lonny doing?"

"Not too well. He's scared and not saying much. He may have given me a lead. Of course, it might also be a dead end."

"Any chance they'll let him out on bail?"

"Sonia's working on getting a hearing on that."

"Do you have enough to pay the bond?"

"Depends how high it is, but I think I can manage."

She couldn't figure out exactly what he was expressing, except that his concern seemed genuine.

"Let me know if you need help."

She nodded, grateful but cautious. Was there a quid pro quo here, the implication of a future payback that she'd missed? Her desire for support won out. For once, she wouldn't try to do it all on her own.

"We'll see about that. Meanwhile, Lonny may have given me a lead about the truck he was driving the night of the murder. Some answers could be at the hatchery, so I plan to go there later today."

Phil didn't hesitate.

"Would you like some company?"

Whatever surprise she felt at his offer disappeared in a sense of relief that she wouldn't be alone.

"Okay. Let's say six o'clock. I need to visit two clients; and, besides, it's the night watchman I want to talk to and he doesn't start until then."

"Call me when you're ready."

Any suspicion she had was gone. She'd get through the afternoon. Deep down, her worries gnawed. But she could also feel a trace of unaccustomed relief.

6:14 PM

Phil looked out of the corner of his eye at Calla unwrapping sandwiches she had bought at Safeway before arriving at his office parking lot ten minutes ago. By mutual agreement, they left her car there and were driving together to the hatchery in his Saab.

Maybe it was also mutual agreement, or its cousin, similar feelings, that encouraged a silence. There was nothing more to say about Lonny until they had more information. He doubted that Calla would want to rehash her afternoon client visits any more than he wanted to talk about trivial tasks at his office. And he felt something new, exciting, maybe unwise and certainly complicating about this trip together.

He'd faithfully loved and, through a virulent cancer, cared for a remarkable woman for fourteen years. When she died, so had any desire to share his life with another person. Not that he hadn't gotten feelers and occasional blatant suggestions from lonely, well-meaning women. Several of them were attractive. But while his mind catalogued their charms, his bruised heart would not open.

Calla, with her beautiful open face and full feminine figure, was definitely on the attractive short list. As his father would have said: built to last, not for show. But Calla had an obvious short-term liability because of Lonny's situation. Probably he should wait until the matter was resolved. Trouble was, he didn't want to wait. Just the thought of *not* going with her to the hatchery this evening made him feel unexpectedly lonely.

Calla's self-conscious posture and the way she looked straight ahead out the windshield made him wonder if she might not be wrestling with similar thoughts. But then, that was probably wishful projection.

They quickly disposed of their turkey and cheese sandwiches as he drove. He finished first and spoke up.

"This Gabby Thibodeau. Do you want to see him alone, or should I come along?"

"Are you asking whether it's safe for me to talk to him alone?"

He forced a soft laugh to keep the conversation light.

"Hardly. From what you told me about your work, seeing him wouldn't come close to cracking your top ten bad moments."

A glance in her direction revealed a tight smile in return.

"You remembered? And here I thought I'd just been boring you."

"Hardly."

Silence again. He knew they'd been riffing and guessed she might have noticed, too.

She didn't take long to break the silence and nodded in decision.

"Come with me, but let me do the talking. With you standing there, I might get better attention. I may be a county official; but to guys like Gabby, I'm still a woman. Easy to ignore. After that, it's best I be on my own with Gabby."

"You got it."

They got out and found Harland Casey standing behind the car. On seeing them, he snapped from a watchful slouch to full height, with a high-wattage smile to match.

"Don't be surprised I always keep an eye out part of the job you undoubtedly know we're closed but that makes no difference because another part of our job Janice and mine is to be of service whenever we're needed so how can I help you Mr. Mayor and Ms....sorry I don't think we've met yet but it will be my distinct pleasure I can assure you."

"Hello, Harland. Harland Casey, Calla Ogden. Ms. Ogden works in social services for the county."

A handshake and a slight bow from Harland.

"Working late, Ms. Ogden. Would you be related to our valued helper Lonny Ogden who now appears to be in a speck of trouble?"

"He's my brother."

Harland's head bobbed rapidly.

"I hope he's all right. We sure like Lonny. How can I help you Ms. Ogden?"

"We'd like to talk to Gabby Thibodeau, your watchman."

"Not mine, you know he works for the hatchery actually for the management which is part BIA, part State, part..."

"But he's here?"

Hesitation.

"Yes."

Harland's wide smile couldn't hide the fact that he was buying time. Phil decided he should help things along.

"Any problem in seeing him right now, Harland?"

Harland looked toward the hatchery gate, rearranged his posture and lost part of his smile.

"There's someone with him now. A policeman with a hard name to pronounce. Russian, maybe. He asked me to go on with any work I had and pay no attention to him. I don't think he'd appreciate being interrupted."

"Would the policeman's name be Takarchuk?"

"Something like that."

"We'll wait. You can go back to what you were doing."

Phil led Calla to a bench, and on the way saw a police car in the far corner of the parking lot. He might have noticed it sooner if Harland had not captured their attention. The man seemed edgier than when they had first met—preoccupied or worried. Harland didn't go back to any job or to his trailer; he sat at another bench, his eyes closed and his face held up to the late sun. Phil didn't buy the relaxed mood that the posture was supposed to convey.

The sun hadn't yet sunk behind the mountains, and pleasant warmth replaced the heat of the day. Nighttime coolness would soon arrive. Calla maintained the silence of someone wrestling with difficult thoughts; he didn't want to intrude.

They didn't have to wait long before Phil heard the sliding gate grind open and saw Greg Takarchuk heading toward his car. When Greg spotted them, he changed direction and approached.

"Enjoying the evening, Mr. Mayor? Not the place I'd have expected to see you."

"Evening, Greg. This is Calla Ogden. She works for the county and is the sister of Lonny Ogden."

Greg stiffened a notch.

"Hello, Ms. Ogden. I saw you around the station. May I ask whether your presence here is related to your brother's case?"

Phil saw Calla grow alert. She flashed a quick glance in his direction before concentrating on Greg.

"Hello, officer. I'm here to find out about a matter that could be important to my brother in case he has to defend himself in court."

"And what would that matter be?"

"The ownership of the truck he was driving on the night of the murder."

Greg hooked his thumbs in his holster belt.

"That information is of major interest to the police. We've done a preliminary check, but the VIN has been scraped and the plates are stolen. If you learn anything about the vehicle, it would be your duty to pass it on to us."

Stress must have gotten to Calla: she raised her voice.

"I'm a public servant like you, and I know the difference between legal requirement and personal responsibility. I'm a responsible person."

Greg softened his approach.

"I'm sure you are, or Mayor Bianchi wouldn't be here with you. I can't stop you from speaking to anyone you want. But if you were to uncover anything about the truck's ownership, would you please tell me?"

"Of course."

Greg's posture relaxed and he modulated the official tone.

"I suppose you'll want to see Thibodeau now. But don't expect much. He played dumb or rambled around my questions. No reason to think he'll be any different with you. But you can try."

"Thanks. I've got other ways to talk to him. You're a policeman, and I can speak as a Native American. Might not work, but we'll see."

As Calla moved away, Phil noticed that Harland was now standing not too far away, leaning in and probably listening. When Calla passed him, Harland fell in step.

"I'll take you to Gabby he's sometimes hard to find not that he doesn't do a good job but it's his way to be invisible, not..."

Phil was pretty sure Harland would try to push himself into any conversation between Calla and Thibodeau, so he moved in close.

"Harland, tell you what. Ms. Ogden's been here before, and she's acquainted with Thibodeau. Let's give her a chance to talk to him alone. You can go back to Janice and your TV shows."

Harland stood still, smile fading. Lengthening shadows had reached his face so Phil could not see his eyes. But everything else about him said he was disturbed. His mouth opened, then shut as he moved toward the trailer with a noticeable woodenness in his gait.

Calla didn't wait. Phil hurried to catch up with her as she approached the hatchery gate and pushed the red entry button.

7:15 PM

A slight figure emerged from the shadows and listlessly approached the gate as if he were being hailed against his will. He slouched to a halt, and Calla got a better look at him. His native features looked familiar, especially when matched with his messy white hair. The clothes that hung on his small frame must have been hand-me-downs or found at a thrift shop.

"Gabby Thibodeau?"

"I recognize you. Seen you at the store at the rez. This place is closed."

Thibodeau looked straight at Phil, standing beside her, as he spoke. Calla raised her voice a notch and succeeded in getting Thibodeau to look at her.

"I know, Gabby. I just want to talk to you."

"What about?"

"Lonny."

"Just talked to a cop. You talk to him. He'll tell you what I said."

"I'd rather ask you myself. Lonny is my brother."

Gabby started to turn away, took his time turning back. His reply was reluctant.

"Okay. Come ahead."

Despite the agreement in his words, the chain link fence still was a solid wall between them.

"Come on, Gabby. Let me in. I won't take long. Just me."

She gestured toward Phil, who gave her an encouraging glance and started back toward the parking lot. Thibodeau muttered under his breath, but finally opened the gate, and walked with her a few yards to where an outdoor fixture was already on, though its illumination wouldn't be necessary for another hour.

She tried a few direct questions about Lonny's work there. At most, Gabby confirmed what she already knew. But he clammed up entirely when she mentioned the truck. So she switched and tried to approach from a different direction.

"You know our history, Gabby. We've been used all the time by others. Used to get what they wanted."

Gabby would know what she meant by "we"—the Native people, Indians, the Yakama in particular. Suspicion still filled his eyes, but maybe a spark of interest, too. She lowered her voice and spoke soothingly.

"In lots of stories, Coyote—*Speel-yi*—is in there. The Trickster usually takes things from people, but sometimes he gives people what look like free gifts. But he's always playing a trick, trying to get something bigger, using all the animals and people he calls friends to get what he wants."

She quoted snippets of well-known stories—about Coyote and Fishhawk, Fox and Eagle, each one making her point from a different slant. Gabby nodded before the conclusion of each tale, showing he knew what was coming. His silence finally broke. He began a fast rasp of short, staccato sentences, as if he were ejecting words he would just as soon be rid of. She saw the anger in his eyes.

"Ya know, Calla, us Indians still get used. You'd think we wouldn't fall for it after all these years. That truck's not mine. Couldn't be. I ain't got the money for it. I just loaned it like it was mine."

"Whose is it?"

"Can't tell."

"You know the police can use the truck to say you had something to do with the murder?"

"I'll take that chance. Other chances'd be worse."

"What other chances?"

"Can't say."

A longer silence followed. Whites, Anglos—they had many names within the native population—generally couldn't abide silence for very long. After a while they had to fill it with words. Native Americans found silence comfortable and could stay inside its bounds for long periods, as if warmed by a familiar blanket. Silence was a safe haven. You could wait within it, preparing yourself before having to confront an alien experience.

Gabby must have been in that in-between space, because when he spoke again, the rasp was gone. Although his voice still sounded low and almost indistinct, it was wrapped in a familiar cadence.

"The old stories, yeah, they speak truths, but not the kind that helps out here."

He gestured vaguely at the hatchery buildings.

"It's not fair, you know."

She had to lean toward him to catch the words; but she did it gradually, trying to be gentle rather than appear probing.

"There's lots of unfairness around, Gabby. Are we talking about the truck?"

"That's part of it."

"Part of what?"

"What shouldn't have happened but did. You know that other story, how the old woman dies when she looks for Owl? She didn't do anything wrong, just looked. Here a person is murdered."

"Does that mean the truck had something to do with the murder?"

Gabby shrank away, his voice turning harsh again.

"Not because of me. All I did was tell Lonny he could use it."

She kept her voice low, countering his nervous rasp with the gentle rhythm of story-telling.

"So someone else owned the truck, but asked you to tell Lonny he could use it?"

Gabby stared mutely at the ground. She took his silence as confirmation. She moved in closer again and spoke just above a whisper.

"Can you tell me who it was?"

He recoiled, shuddered, and moved a long step back, closing the subject with a single projectile word that matched his rigid posture.

"No!"

She backed away from the outburst.

"All right, Gabby. I understand. But maybe you can help me a little. If I wanted to find out who owns the truck, where would I look? You don't need to say anything, just nod."

He stared stonily before responding with a slight movement of his chin.

She recited, speaking slowly and pausing after each designation.

"The rez ... the Haynes farm ... the service station where the murder happened."

No nod to any of them.

"Here at the hatchery."

A barely perceptible nod. Her breath caught in her throat.

"The hatchery management and crew?"

Gabby stood stock still, staring away from her. She saw the barest negative shake of his head. But before she had a chance to say more, he walked away, fading into the lengthening shadows that were gradually attaching themselves to the buildings.

She was able to open the gate from the inside. As she heard it closing behind her, she approached Phil and Officer Takarchuk. They stopped talking and turned toward her.

Without waiting to be asked, she recounted her conversation with Gabby. Takarchuk asked the first question.

"So he confirmed that the owner of the truck is someone connected with the hatchery, but not on the actual staff?"

"Not in so many words, but he implied both those things."

Takarchuk was silent for a minute. When he spoke again, it was as if he were thinking out loud.

"That leaves only a couple of candidates, one obvious."

She was thinking the same thing.

DAY THREE

2:48 AM

Two hours before first light, Jason paced five steps along the length of his living room, back two, four more into the computer room, made an about face, retraced his steps, and slumped into a chair. He'd been making that short round trip off and on over the five hours since darkness seeped into his unlit home.

His concentration was shattered. His brain and body felt like they were falling down a deep hole with no bottom. And why? Just because he had met his sister and little Jace and spent most of a day with them. Doing nothing. Just watching, saying little, hearing Lila's soft encouragements to little Jace and his bouncing enthusiasm in reply.

He had stayed until Lila got ready to leave for her job at the bar. She relaxed with Jace, while shyly revealing a combination of need and happiness over his return into her life. But when it was time to go to work, resigned lethargy took over. Her auto-pilot, slow-motion departure routine was laced with sadness, and he became intensely aware of the dirt and disorder in the house.

She tried to make a casual admission, but could not hide her discomfort and shame.

"I got into drugs. I'm four months clean now. I stayed away from them while I was pregnant and I cut way back after Jace came. But I go back and forth. It's hard. I try to stop for Jace's sake. But being alone and all ..."

She pointed toward the pigsty of a living room, avoiding eye contact. He had already guessed, his heart rate rising as he simultaneously acknowledged to himself that some of her drugs might have reached her indirectly through him. Probably had. When he was actively distributing, there were few local users that didn't get eventually some of their supply through him.

Lila and Jace floated nearby in his imagination, out of focus. The computer glowed bright in front of him, with Lila's admission of drug use wrapped around it like white noise. He was stuck in indecision, conscious of a new feeling. Something to do with happiness? He tried imagining everything in color, not his usual black and gray.

92

As he drifted, an idea formed. He'd already thought about getting away from the drug game. Could he do the same for Lila and Jace—get *them* away? With a start, he realized he was actually thinking about helping someone else. That had never happened before. The alien realization that he might be capable of being responsible for someone else felt like a vise squeezing his heart. He'd heard people talk about the weight of responsibility. But if wanting to protect Lila and Jace would weigh him down, how come he also felt strangely lighter?

He'd try to figure that one out later. Right now, a different realization took over, like an eighteen wheeler coming at him down a one-lane road. It was his past, and all the damage it could do if it ran him over. Up to now, his thoughts about getting away, getting out from under, had been just speculation. Now he realized that he'd already made the decision to get out, and stay out permanently.

But how would Lila and Jace factor in that decision? At least he knew a location where he could take them, where he and Lila could bury their pasts. What he didn't know was whether Lila wanted change or protection enough to come along. He warned himself: don't let imagination lead the way. Take everything in order. Deal with what needs doing right now, then see what happens and deal with that. That method had always worked before. No reason it would fail now.

So what did he have?

Actual information about the murder? No. What he did have was some knowledge about the new drug, Salvation, along with hints from internet traffic that the drug might be tied to the killing. He'd begin by going deeper with that idea, to see if people with previous access to Salvation might have reason to kill Rolf. He'd build himself a cache of information that the cops didn't have. With such information he might be able to bargain. Without a bargaining position, he'd still be on a suspect list and it would be harder to get away. Or impossible.

He sat upright, then stood and, like a dog emerging from water, shook himself all over, each leg and each arm separately, agitating them until they began to hurt. When he stopped, his whole body tingled and his brain was back online. Ready, he went to his computers.

For the next hour, he reviewed files he had kept of internet chatter from the past year. For many months, he'd carefully reviewed messages that came in on a daily basis, and had saved information that he thought would be of future use. He was limited to information from computers on which he had installed Trojan horses and would be ignoring many more messages he did not have access to. His was just a sampling of information, but, he was sure, from an information base large enough to give him what he wanted.

He began by looking for new messages originating in Kittinach County that commented on the murder or mentioned Salvation. As he worked, his area of geographic interest quickly expanded to most of Central Washington, and included parts of Seattle and Bellingham.

He paid attention to when emails about Salvation appeared, and soon discovered particular locations, or clusters of messages that were exchanged at the same time periods. Sometimes time and location coincided. It looked as if the interest in Salvation had moved from place to place in a regular pattern.

He tried another approach, aggregating in a single massive file all the messages that he thought contained relevant information. Then he searched for dates and places he'd noted more than once. Most of the dates he searched for fell into the period May 1 to September 30. Places from which the emails originated clustered around Swiftwater and Bellingham, with a smaller subset in greater Seattle.

He ran individual names against the total email volume, creating lists of high, medium, and low frequency email users. Some people always wrote more or less than others, so volume by itself didn't tell him much. But by analyzing usual patterns he could look for anomalies: time periods when individuals wrote and/or received more mail than usual.

Once the email analysis was done, he repeated the same process with a large general collection of recent text messages.

When he finally merged both information sets, he teased out all individuals who had written or received at least one message that directly or obliquely mentioned the drug trade, and ran those names against the individuals who had popped up when he looked for volume anomalies. As the final results came up on his screen, Jason knew he would have either a short list of names to investigate further, or he would have nothing.

Six names stood out. The first, Sonny Rolf, the murder victim, he eliminated for obvious reasons. The second was a man who he knew had gone back to prison three months ago. Three other people he recognized immediately: Lonny Ogden, Terry Haynes, and Bill McHugh. The last, Gabby Thibodeau, was a man he'd vaguely heard of.

Ogden and Haynes were minor players. Both had been or still were users, and fit at some low level into the distribution chain. Ogden, of course, was a suspect in Rolf's killing; but he wondered whether Ogden was smart and organized enough to have done the job. Frankly, he didn't give a shit either way. He didn't care who the murderer was. All he wanted was to get his own name off the suspect list.

McHugh, the obsessive bastard who had hounded him for years, might be dirty, but so what? Or McHugh could be on his short list of suspects for the simple reason that, as the cop who worked most on drug cases, attention to his activities generated a lot of traffic.

Thibodeau was the one he needed to find out more about. All Jason knew was his name and, from the email traffic, that he'd recently been active in the drug scene. So he was a player. But at what level? The man couldn't be too high up, or Jason would have noticed him long ago.

That was enough computer work for now. A physical sweep of his house would be a kind of relief from so much mental strain. He was very confident about his home security system, an impregnable network of sensors, locks, and alarms. He also vacuumed his house from top to bottom once a week, removing everything from the shelves and paying particular attention to places where dust could accumulate, like floor corners and drawers. This weekly cleaning was a ritual he enjoyed in its own right; it reinforced his sense of order. Besides, it kept his machinery clean, and gave him a chance to toss items before they became clutter.

He began now with a random spot check of the house and, finding nothing, moved on to the garage. Security was not so robust there, but it didn't need to be. Everything seemed in order. His car looked undisturbed too, right down to the floor mats. Until he opened the glove compartment.

His hand froze in midair. In the glow of the dome light he could see little clods or crumbs of some kind in one corner of the compartment. Someone must have put them there. Someone had gotten into his garage.

Bright red anger rose inside him; he had to douse it with a bucket of cold discipline. Who could have done this? He knew immediately. Only one person had ever been in his house, and that person must have returned.

Officer Greg Fuckin' Takarchuk.

6:00 AM

Greg was already at his desk, and for the next hour wrote up a report of his visit to the hatchery the evening before. He summarized Calla Ogden's input and added a carefully-worded assessment that Thibodeau might still be hiding information vital to the investigation. It was not his job to decide whether the watchman should be brought in for questioning, but he hoped that Espy and McHugh might see it that way. He emailed the report to them, and a copy to Chief Cisek.

He intended to use the day ahead to follow up on two matters. The two men who had been in a bar with Lonny on the evening of the murder had reported that Lonny met another male there and talked with him for about two minutes. Lonny claimed he was so wasted that he couldn't remember the encounter, much less who the person was. It was possible that those two men might have seen more than they realized, but he'd save them for the afternoon since it was unlikely the barflies would be stirring before then.

He would use the morning to visit Jason Ferris again. For one thing, Jason had been cooperative. For another, there was no escaping the fact that even if he were not connected to the murder, Jason had once been, and still might be, involved with the local drug scene. The killing was tied to that unusual drug called Salvation. Jason was obviously smart, and if he felt like cooperating further he might be willing to point the police toward the source of Salvation. It was definitely a long shot, but worth a try.

At 8:30 am, he drove toward Portal. A dome of thick clouds made the sky feel lower than yesterday's expansive blue cover. By afternoon, the overcast might break up and let bright sunlight through again. Or it might decide to stay for a few days. There were two things you knew about weather in the mountains: one, change was coming; and two, beyond that you knew nothing. Not unlike the current investigation: opaque for sure, with uncertainty about whether there would be any break soon.

A few minutes later, he knocked on Jason Ferris' front door. To one side he thought he saw a slight movement behind the partially-cracked louvered shutters over a window. But when he looked for further movement, he saw none. He made a slow circuit around the garage and yard then returned to the front porch, where he knocked again. Neither hearing nor seeing a response, he raised his voice and addressed the door.

"It's Greg Takarchuk, Jason. The information you gave me checked out and, as far as I know, you're no longer a suspect. But I have some new information I wanted to talk to you about. Come on, you can trust me."

He heard the sound of door chains being removed and relaxed. So much for the warning about the uncooperative Jason. Might not be such a bad guy as McHugh believed. The door opened an inch or so and he heard Jason's voice.

"Trust you? Eat shit!"

The words burst from the narrow opening like hot venom. Greg took an involuntary step back. What was that about? He dialed in the calmness he was trained to use in situations like this.

"I thought we were beyond that kind of talk, Jason. What happened?"

"As if you didn't know, Mr. Cool Cop. You got balls. But then, pretending is what you're all about."

"I don't have any idea what you're talking about."

The door slammed shut. He waited a minute, then pounded on the door and called out again.

No response, so he tore a page from his note pad and wrote: "Salvation's tied to the murder. Can you give anything that would help the investigation?" He pushed the note under the door. A moment later, it came back with a large "X" through his words and a scrawled, "fuck you".

He turned away for a moment, looking across town at the cone-shaped tailings hill from one of the oldest mines. Calmed, he turned back to Jason's door and tried once more.

"Okay, I know you're mad and I don't know why, but I'll leave you alone. Here's my card again, with my cell, in case you change your mind."

He pushed his card under the door, then thought of one more thing. Still stooped over, he shouted at the bottom of the door, imagining Jason just on the other side, hoping his words could slip under the thick oak.

"A piece of advice. You might be better off telling me whatever happened to upset you. I might be able to help you like you helped me."

He left and, once back in his car, called Espy and gave him a neutral account of the encounter, ending with a comment on Jason's mood.

"Jason's very mad about something. Not sure what it is, though."

"He give you any particulars?"

"Only that he thinks that whatever happened, I was in on it. Anyway, I doubt he'll be of help to us anymore."

He waited, and only heard Espy's low breathing. His reply, when it came, was casual; but Greg thought he heard tension at the edges.

"Interesting, I guess. Let me know right away if you hear more on that."

"You got it. I thought I'd go now to check on the guys who were with Lonny at the bar the night of the murder. Probably a dead end, but I'll let you know if I find out anything."

"Do that."

11:50 AM

Trapped in a filthy mobile home for the time being, Calla had to push down the sense of irritation rising within her. For fifteen minutes she had been trying to get 84-year-old Ada Gwen to agree to a visit by the county nurse.

A part of her irritation was directed at herself. She was usually well prepared to address her clients, their differing needs and circumstances. But Lonny's situation had thrown her off. She had only half concentrated when she reviewed the file on Ada before making her visit.

While Ada considered her decision, Calla tried to relax. She'd once been at a course on relaxation and memory. Though applying the exact techniques she was taught usually ended up making her tenser, she did find that if she could relax, information she sought occurred to her more easily. Through a smeared trailer window she focused on green trees in a stray patch of sunlight. She imagined lying under the trees, a young Lonny bounding happily around her.

After a minute, she returned her attention to Ada; and the pinched features and unwashed, lank hair of Ada's granddaughter, Michelle, replaced Lonny in her imagination. Michelle was supposed to be taking care of her elderly relative. Instead, she used the trailer as free housing, was often absent, and partied hard. Frail Ada had to search for food in a kitchen that Michelle restocked when she felt like it rather than when her grandmother needed provisions.

Ada still looked downward, stooped and silent. Calla couldn't wait any longer.

"Ada, I hate to put it this way, but your life won't get better until Michelle moves out and moves on. Right now this place is just a convenience for her. She's using drugs again, and using you."

The old lady raised her head.

"Okay, Calla. Tell the nurse to come. But don't think she can come all the time. Just this once."

That's all she got, but Calla felt better for being able to check off one item on her long to-do list, and for seeing at least one person take a tentative step forward. She thanked Ada, exited the trailer, and crossed the road to her car, parked near the trees she had glimpsed through the trailer window.

Next to them was what looked to have once been a farm. Clouds dominated from above, but not enough of them to bring rain to a browning landscape that, only a month ago, had been too water-logged to plant. Just like the pendulum of her own life, she thought: either too wet or too dry.

Today the pendulum felt somewhere near a midpoint. Objectively, she didn't have that much new to go on. Lonny was still in jail. But when you're deep in despair, even a little hope, like stray sunshine, can seem like a lot.

A thought occurred to her. Lonny evidently got some pleasure, and maybe a little hope, from the kindnesses that Janice Casey extended to him. Her next appointment was not until 1:30 pm, and she had time to drive to the hatchery and thank Janice personally.

12:05 PM

Just after noon, Greg parked the department's Ford Explorer in a lot at The Wayside, an isolated bar between the Yakama Reservation and the interstate. A faded sign on top of a high pole beside the road announced the bar's name. Apparently the place had once been a dwelling, then possibly a gas station. A concrete island where gas pumps might have stood was now home to a planter. Shriveled low bushes, barely alive in the dry dirt, said all that was needed about general upkeep.

The same was true of the dim interior of the place. Furnishings were as listless as the few patrons seated at tables in the shadows or bellied up to the slab bar, a thick plank set on saw horses. The room smelled of old sweat, beer, and dust.

But he got lucky. A pot-bellied bartender in a dirty Harley shirt silently pointed to one table, when Greg mentioned the men he was looking for. He approached the table and two hunched men, probably in their twenties, came into focus. Both wore jeans and dark long-sleeve T-shirts. One wore a baseball cap.

"Jack Avery and Al Toms?"

One face looked up. Round, crooked nose, wide eyes, color not identifiable in the bar's twilight, lank dark hair hanging down from the edges of the cap.

"Who are you?"

"Officer Greg Takarchuk, Swiftwater and Portal."

He pulled out his badge.

Round face spoke again.

"Not your jurisdiction."

This would not be the man's first encounter with the law.

"I'm not after you. Just want information. Are you Avery or Toms?"

A pause. The face turned down toward the table, then back up again.

"Toms. Information about what?"

Greg pulled a chair from the next table and sat down.

"In a minute. First, I need your friend to identify himself."

The other head lifted enough to show a face. Very pale freckled skin and light eyes surrounded by a fringe of sandy hair appeared for a moment before disappearing again. Greg barely heard the mumbled reply.

"Avery."

Toms would do the talking and confirmed as much.

"He don't say much ever."

"You both know about the murder of Sonny Rolf. And, according to a report I read, you both met with Lonny Ogden in this bar the night of the murder."

Toms held up a hand.

"Not when you put it that way. We were here. Lonny came in and sat at that next table there. We don't hang with him much. Said hello. Maybe just nodded."

"Can you describe what he wore?"

Toms half sneered.

"As if we care. Stupid hat he always wears with lots of colors—all I remember."

"The report said it was your opinion that he was drunk or stoned. That his voice was slurred. So you must have said more than 'hi' to each other."

"Heard him talk to the waitress and he sounded pretty wasted. Later, anyway."

"What do you mean by 'later'?"

"After he met the guy at the bar."

"Tell me about that."

Toms sat up straighter.

"What's goin' on? You think Lonny did the murder?"

"Do you?"

"The fuck do I care."

Why should he? His bored druggie eyes were incapable of interest in anything but the next fix.

"Okay. Back to the guy at the bar. Can you describe him?"

"Didn't pay that much attention. Small dude, though."

"How long was Lonny with him?"

"Don't know. Wasn't watchin' that much. Maybe a minute, maybe five. Not like a half hour or anything like that."

"Then what happened?"

"The guy at the bar left. Then Lonny came back to his table."

"What time was that?"

"Dunno. Maybe after midnight. We already told that to the other cop."

Toms threw a glance Avery's way and got no response.

"Anything else?"

"Naw. Not really."

Avery suddenly spoke without moving his head, his words again barely audible.

"Lonny started eating something."

Greg flipped his notebook open.

"Right away?"

"Naw, after a while."

"Could you see what it was?"

"Naw."

Toms mulled something over.

"He ordered another drink and that's when he sounded slurred. But he could've been high or something."

Time for the most important question.

"How long after the guy at the bar left did Lonny leave?"

Toms, again.

"Maybe a half hour. Could have been longer."

"Thanks, guys."

He got up to leave, and they offered no reaction. He didn't bother talking to the male bartender, since the person tending bar on the night of the murder had been a female. He stepped back into an overcast afternoon that hit him like full sunlight, compared to the gloomy bar.

He was reaching for his cell to see if the secretary at the station had an address for that female bartender when the phone buzzed.

"Takarchuk."

"Ferris. Wanna talk."

He barely recognized the low grumble. It was like part of Jason wanted to talk but was battling another part of him that resisted.

"When?"

"I'm at home now."

Finding the other bartender would have to wait.

"Forty minutes."

He drove over the speed limit back to Portal, letting his mind roam over what he had learned in the bar.

Two things stood out. Lonny had always claimed that he blacked out in his truck and slept through the time of the murder. The person at the bar could have given him something that knocked him out. Whoever that person was, he was small, and only one small person kept showing up on the radar.

First Jason. Then he would take a closer look at Gabby Thibodeau.

His cell rang but cut off when he answered. The call came from the dispatcher, and Greg punched "reply".

"Greg here."

"Chief wants you at the hatchery. Now. We've got another dead body."

Jason would have to wait.

12:17 PM

The drive ate up only twelve minutes. Calla parked and walked over to the only person in sight: a lady with a crutch tending to flower vines growing on a trellis.

"Mrs. Casey? I'm Calla Ogden, Lonny's sister."

The woman carefully returned her pruning shears to a canvas bag at her feet and turned to face Calla, holding out the hand that wasn't clutching a crutch.

"Pleased to meet you, Calla. Lonny mentioned you a lot. Call me Janice. Let's go over there."

Janice raised her crutch to point at a bench on the edge of the grass semi-circle, and led the way in a gait that was more lurch than hobble. Once seated, it was evident how much such determined movement cost her. Calla watched her breathing slow down as she straightened and flicked back a strand of gray-brown hair that had fallen over her eyes.

At a distance, she would have put Janice in her late fifties, a bit older than Calla's mother would have been if she had lived. But up close, she revised that estimate downward. Though ravages had aged the face and body, Janice's eyes and surprisingly smooth skin belonged to someone ten years younger.

"Your brother is a sweet young man. Still seems like a confused kid sometimes, but a good heart."

She was relieved by the succinct and accurate description. It sounded as if this woman had seen Lonny more accurately than so many people who dismissed him as a twitchy weirdo.

"I'm grateful for the kindness you showed him."

"No work at all. Just some snacks and stories."

"So you know how much Lonny likes stories?"

"After we met, he asked if I knew any. So I pulled out the old fairy tales—Jack and the Beanstalk, Sleeping Beauty, you know. Probably didn't get them right, but it didn't matter. A story's a story."

Janice paused and went on with a new note of concern.

"I hope he's okay. Can't imagine how he's taken those nights in jail, a restless person like him."

"It's been hard on him."

Their conversation reached a dead end quicker than she expected, and she was not sure what she could get from further small talk. Without any sort of plan, she began asking questions.

"Did he ever tell you that he knew Rolf, the man who was murdered? Or that he was supplying Rolf with drugs?"

"No to both of those questions. Though I heard his motorcycle going out at night several times—I'm a real light sleeper—and I didn't ask what he was doing. Maybe he had this completely different life I didn't know about, and maybe he dealt in drugs. But murder doesn't fit with him."

Calla nodded at the familiar conclusion.

"How well did he know Gabby Thibodeau?"

"Good question. They had plenty of time at night to talk. But I can't say for sure whether they did. I've never trusted Gabby and have said as much to my husband—several times. There's something shifty about Gabby, like, if you'll excuse me ..."

Janice adjusted her torso and threw a glance in Calla's direction.

"... like some Indians. Not like all Indians—I know about your and Lonny's heritage—but some."

Calla was well aware of the quicksand in Janice's statement, but this was not the time to explore that terrain.

"You think Gabby might have been a bad influence on Lonny?"

She thought of the fear in Lonny's eyes when she had mentioned the Stick-showers.

"Can't say for sure, but if you want a straight guess, I'd say, yes."

Calla nodded. So far, she'd learned nothing she didn't already know or couldn't have guessed. She could tell Janice was tiring; so she decided not to bother the poor woman further. She held out her hand, taking leave, and Janice responded with a firm, calloused grip.

"I appreciate your time, and again, all you did for Lonny. You may have helped him once more in being so candid with me."

On the way back to her car, she turned her cell phone on. A message had come in from Sonia D'Amico: the judge had granted Lonny's request for bail. He would be ready to be picked up soon.

Elated, she opened her car door. She'd call Phil, then drive back toward Swiftwater. Over her shoulder, she saw Janice talking agitatedly into a cell phone, and heard the sound of a car approaching at high speed. Moments later, a police car rounded the corner and, instead of stopping at the parking lot, pulled up in front of the lowered vehicle barrier to the hatchery.

Greg Takarchuk jumped out of his car and rushed around the barrier into the hatchery compound. Janice stood up from the bench and advanced a few paces, visibly unsteady.

Calla hurried over to her.

"What is it, Janice?"

"The call. They found Gabby Thibodeau dead back where Lonny used to sleep. Harland found him. That was him on the phone. He's afraid."

"About what?"

"That they'll find out he was in prison before. He's always been afraid of that."

There was a lot more she wanted to ask, but all she could think about was getting to Lonny.

"Will you be all right?"

"You mean, can I take care of myself? I've been through worse."

Bitterness formed a sheath around the resolve in Janice's answer.

12:47 PM

Greg ran across the main hatchery area, heading toward the metal building where he had twice inspected Lonny Ogden's makeshift sleeping quarters. Chief Cisek had called a moment ago: the body belonged to Gabby Thibodeau. Ahead of him he could see a knot of people. Greg recognized the hatchery manager—a large Yakama with a black-haired ponytail—and two other hatchery staff members. Beside them stood the tall swaying figure of Harland Casey.

As Greg hurried toward the group, he reconsidered his priorities. Investigation of Thibodeau's actions on the night of Rolf's murder was now on hold. He still had to talk to the night bartender at The

Wayside. That would have to wait, but something else couldn't wait. Right after the dispatcher's call, he'd phoned Jason as he drove, explaining that something had come up and that he would have to postpone their conversation. He had heard echoes of his own vague excuse in Jason's curt, disinterested response. He wasn't sure that Jason would ever agree to talk again. For now, he had to focus on the situation at hand.

He spoke to the manager as he came to a halt.

"Tell me what happened."

The hatchery manager remained taciturn, responding softly. A few paces behind him, Harland Casey's anxious face peered in.

"No one was looking for Gabby. We assumed he'd gone home early. Mr. Casey reported finding Gabby's motorcycle behind the shed, where we hadn't seen it. Then he found the body in the shed, about a half hour ago. I confirmed that and called the police."

"Has anyone gone back into the shed since then?"

The manager glanced in the direction of the shed, shook his head, kept his voice low.

"We know better than to do that."

Greg realized his abruptness might have sounded like an implication of incompetence.

"Didn't mean to suggest otherwise. Thank you for your quick response. Go ahead back to your normal work. We'll call you if we need anything more."

The manager raised his hand in acceptance and walked back toward the administrative building. Greg could now focus on Casey.

Casey was sweating much more than the clouded skies required.

"Okay, Mr. Casey. Take me through what happened."

"Janice and I emptied the trash and vacuumed in the Visitors' Center until about noon. We usually eat lunch around 12:45. I thought I'd get out the push lawnmower to mow the grass after lunch. I came to this shed here, saw the cycle, then went in for the mower. The door to the closet where Lonny slept was open. They keep mostly winter and rain gear in there and I knew Lonny was in jail, so I went over to close the door and looked inside and there was Gabby."

There was no rush of words this time. Casey's recitation sounded, if anything, calm and rehearsed.

"Then what did you do?"

"I thought he might be asleep. I shook him by the arm and felt how cold his skin was. He didn't move. So I went to the office and told the director. He came back here with me, saw Gabby and called you guys."

"Okay. Let's have a look."

The inside of the building looked the same as Greg remembered from his previous visits. None of the stored equipment seemed out of place. Inside the space where Lonny had slept, Gabby Thibodeau lay chest down on the grubby mattress, his face turned to one side, elbows extended, and arms paralleling the side of his head. A worn khaki blanket loosely covered his legs. Except for the paleness of his skin and the smell of his loosened bowels, he seemed asleep. Greg looked carefully around the body and at the area outside the door, and saw nothing unusual. A forensic specialist would arrive soon for a more thorough evaluation. Greg led Casey back out to the main hatchery area.

"The tech will be here any minute. Meanwhile, tell me what you did last night."

Casey was still in recitation mode.

"We, Janice and me, had dinner as usual and watched TV until about 10:30. She went to bed and I walked around the place."

"Was that usual?"

"Most nights, yeah. Not part of our job description, but I do it partly to get fresh air, partly to see if everything's normal."

"And was it last night?"

"Completely. At the fence I saw Gabby walking around inside, saw his flashlight, called him over. We talked."

"About what?"

"Weather, mostly. Just small talk."

"And he seemed all right?"

"Same as usual."

"How about this morning? Anything out of place?"

"Not that I saw."

"How about during the night? Did you hear anything?"

Casey thought for a moment and shook his head.

Greg looked down at his brown boots and reflected. Aside from Casey sounding more controlled than usual, he heard nothing suspicious. And he figured he'd reached the end of that subject.

"While we're at it, I wanted to ask you about something else. The night of Rolf's murder, Lonny Ogden was found in a Ford 150 pickup. Before he died, Gabby said that you might know about the ownership of the vehicle and why Lonny was driving it that evening."

Not quite true, but close enough. He had nothing to lose by rattling the cage a little.

Casey looked wildly around before trying unsuccessfully to restore his salesman's smile. He pressed one hand against his hip and shoved the other in a pocket to stop its trembling.

Greg was about to dig into that reaction when a dark SUV with the sheriff's emblem on the door pulled up. McHugh and the forensic tech got out. The tech immediately pulled out a large aluminum case from the back seat.

"All right, Mr. Casey, we'll continue this conversation later. I have to talk to these officers. Please stay where you are."

McHugh impatiently listened to Greg's summary of the situation. The tech, head down and his body language speaking bored disinterest, chewed gum.

McHugh was in charge now. When Greg recounted his conversation with Casey, he saw McHugh glare sharply at the man. Casey was alternating between looking apprehensively their way and trying to pretend he didn't care. When Greg finished his account, McHugh gave terse orders, offering no indication of whether he was satisfied.

"Let's get this done. Takarchuk, bring Casey with you, but stay outside the shed. Stand by in case we have questions."

Then, heading into the hatchery compound, McHugh called back to the tech.

"Do what you have to, and let's get on to the other place."

Not knowing how long it would be before McHugh returned, Greg ushered Casey toward an enclosure that held circulation equipment for the large fish tanks. They sat on a waist-high concrete wall.

Casey bowed forward, upper body uncharacteristically still, long legs hanging down and twitching occasionally. Greg gave Casey a few minutes to settle down, then cleared his throat.

"While we wait, let's go back to the truck."

No response. He added firmness and tried again.

"You'll have to answer my questions sooner or later. Why not start now?"

"No comment. Nothing to say."

"I'm afraid that's not good enough. Look at it this way. If you know nothing about the truck, you might as well say so. If you know something, it's better not to look like you're hiding information."

"Nothing to say."

"You know we'll have to take you to the station for questioning."

That statement produced only a visible shudder.

Greg reminded himself that he was only helping; he was not the officer in charge. So he settled on waiting for McHugh before going further. About twenty minutes later, McHugh emerged from the equipment shed and walked briskly toward them.

"We found a three-inch raised welt on the victim's head and it could have been made by one of the tools in there. We're going to need to fingerprint you, Mr. Casey; and chances are we'll get a warrant to search your truck and trailer along with the rest of the premises. Any comment?"

Casey's fixed stare widened, reflecting resignation more than surprise. He sagged down farther and said nothing.

McHugh wasn't finished.

"We also found what looks like a needle entry point on the victim's right triceps. Confirming that will be the medical examiner's business, but do you want to say anything about it, Mr. Casey?"

After more silence in return, McHugh wrapped things up.

"Takarchuk, you'll need to take Casey down to the Swiftwater station for questioning. Let the Chief know I'll be asking for a warrant to look at the Casey truck and trailer. You'll have to take Mrs. Casey with you. We want her out of the trailer as soon as possible."

Greg waited for more. McHugh finally signaled him to another big tank some distance away from Casey.

"I know I should be running him in myself. But we were on our way somewhere else that could be more important."

McHugh didn't wait for a reaction before continuing.

"We have a lead on Jason Ferris and a warrant to search his garage and car. That's where we're going now. Bagging Ferris is just as big as solving this murder. We could finally start shutting down the whole drug operation out here."

A man on a mission, doing his job, replaced McHugh's usual sour cop attitude. But there was more. McHugh seemed actually happy. Greg recognized that mood immediately: McHugh's enthusiasm for bagging Ferris trumped everything else. It could also have the effect of distorting his judgments about other evidence.

The tech emerged from the shed and stood off to one side, weight on one hip, waiting for orders. McHugh pointed at their SUV and the two men hurried to it. The vehicle executed a tight U-turn and sped away.

Casey stayed where he was, his whole body projecting dejection. Greg wasn't sure that Casey could have run away even if he had wanted to.

"You heard McHugh, Mr. Casey. I've got to take you in."

Casey resignedly moved his arms behind his back and Greg waived him off.

"No need for that right now."

Still, Casey's reaction could be significant: this was not the first time he had executed this drill. Greg almost had to pull Casey to the nearby police Explorer and help him up into the rear seat.

"Wait here. I'm going to get your wife."

As Greg climbed the trailer steps to retrieve Janice Casey, the door opened. Janice held a large purse, as if she had known what was bound to happen. Her head was up and, despite her crutch, she stood straighter than normal: the stoic wife. Silently, she locked the trailer and gave Greg the key at his request. He promised that she would get it back when a search was completed.

They were halfway to the Explorer when his phone rang. He motioned Janice to wait and took a few steps to the side before punching on.

"Couldn't do it yourself, could you. Got that fucker McHugh to come instead."

Jason Ferris, mad as hell.

"Hello, Jason."

"Cut the polite crap. They're tearing up my place, not that you didn't know."

"Until McHugh told me he was on his way, no I didn't."

"Don't bullshit me."

"Where are you?"

"I can see them, they can't see me. All you need to know."

"Look, Jason, I don't have time to talk. But I think we should. You may not believe me, but I don't like some of the things that are going on. I've not been trying to screw you over. I have no need to."

A long silence. Greg had to break it.

"I meant what I said, Jason. I gotta go. Make up your mind."

More of a wait, until …

"I'll call you again. That'll be the last chance."

The line went dead.

Now he had another problem. He could get Harland Casey to the station. But he couldn't commit to babysitting Janice Casey without taking a risk that Jason would call and want to meet. No one else at the station would be able to look after Janice. She was his responsibility, unless he could come up with another solution.

He observed Janice, now listing over her crutch, her bravado giving way to physical strain. He might try social services, but he really needed someone he could trust. So he phoned the only person he could think of who might be able to help him out on short notice.

Phil Bianchi.

1:47 PM

Greg's call did it, Phil realized. He couldn't leave Swiftwater right now.

He walked into the outer office and asked his secretary to cancel his attendance tomorrow at a meeting of Washington mayors in

Seattle. The subject of the meeting was important, though—how greater municipal cooperation could help counteract a looming state budgetary shortfall. He'd submit ideas later in writing.

Secretly, he was glad for an excuse to stay. He couldn't say exactly how his presence might help Calla with Lonny, but a part of him just wanted to be near her.

All Greg had asked was for him to look after Janice Casey for the next few hours. Or find someone who could look after her. Offhand, Phil couldn't come up with anyone he could impose on. Now that the Seattle trip was off, there was no reason he couldn't do the job himself. No reason, he finally admitted, unless that meant not being with Calla. An obvious idea occurred.

He punched in her cell number and she answered right away.

"Hi, Phil. Lonny's being processed now, and I should be able to take him away in about half an hour."

"That's great. I'm free of that trip to Seattle I told you about. I was hoping to see you and Lonny, but something else has come up."

He told her what Greg had asked him to do, without giving away why Janice needed looking after.

"So I guess I'll use that extra time to keep an eye on Janice, unless you have any better suggestions."

Calla didn't think long.

"When Lonny's out, let's all get together. He likes Janice and would be comfortable with her. And you and I could have a chance to talk."

Everything about the day brightened.

"That would be great. Where?"

"Well, there's a private dining room at the Sunrise. I bet we could get them to let us use it."

He hesitated. He didn't want to overreach. Why was a simple arrangement making his stomach feel funny? He tried to make his next words casual.

"That would be okay, I guess. But it's pretty confining. No windows, either. Not a place I'd like to be if I just got out of jail. How about my place? It's just up the hill, and there's a bed where Lonny could lie down if he's tired."

"Sure!"

Enthusiasm lit up her reply and she went right on.

"Have you got food in case I need to fix some for Lonny?"

"For a bachelor, I do actually keep a decent larder. Tell you what: I'll wait here for Janice's arrival. You take Lonny to the lot by City Hall and we'll caravan to my place."

He tried to concentrate on paperwork until Greg called. Minutes later he was at the elevator door on his floor, and led Greg and Janice to his office. Once Janice was seated, Greg brought him up to date in the hallway.

"Harland Casey's at the station, held for questioning. A warrant to search the Casey trailer is being expedited. Someone will let you know when that's finished and Mrs. Casey can go back."

Greg clapped him on the shoulder.

"Thanks for help on short notice, Phil. I mean it. But right now I really gotta go."

Greg disappeared into the elevator and Phil stepped back into his office. He guessed that he might have to keep an eye on Janice Casey for longer than he'd expected. Greg was clearly not going to be back for a while. Janice had shifted her chair so she could look out the window. With clouds masking the mountains, there wasn't much more than the traffic on Main Street to catch your eye. Her head didn't move, even at the sound he made returning to the chair behind his desk.

He tried small talk, and got little more than dull monosyllabic acknowledgments. Only when he explained that Lonny would join them later did a fleeting look of pleasure light her face, before silence took over again.

2:30 PM

Greg stopped at Pioneer Park. After turning over Harland and Janice, he decided not to go back to the station, in order to avoid the possibility of getting sucked into something else. He needed to be free in case Jason Ferris called. That was half an hour ago. He'd give

Jason another half hour. That was as long as he could stretch it before at least checking in with the Chief again.

With his brain slowed for a few minutes, Olga was right there in his thoughts. It was nighttime in Cairo, but he knew that, just after midnight, she would probably still be awake.

He felt the way he had at crunch time, late in a game with a lot on the line. With the clock running down, he had wanted the ball. But having to make a decision about Olga's visit, and perhaps their entire relationship, was far more important than winning or losing a game.

Yes, she was far away. Yes, every day apart from her was hard. That was a simple fact. So was the fact that the murder investigation was heating up. Deep down, he knew that he'd be desolate if he gave up on Olga now, *just* because of temporary job responsibilities. What was the relationship worth to him? It could be a lot or a little, a voice within him answered. But you won't know if you don't have the courage to take it as far as you can.

Determination formed solidly, almost physically, in front of him. If he had to, he'd find a way to spend time with her. He missed her, all of her: beautiful eyes, inquisitive and observant mind, and slim, athletic body.

She sounded fully awake when she answered in Cairo.

He broke through her greeting.

"I want you to come. Please tell me you'll come."

She took her time in replying.

"From tepid to hot, from unsure to sure. Why the change?"

"Because I finally had a chance to think about what's important."

Another pause, not so long.

"But you still have to think before knowing? Will that always be the case?"

You never got off easy with Olga. But now he was sure.

"That's what we need to find out, and we can't find out without being together. One thing I don't have to think about is that I miss you and would like you to be here right now."

The pause that followed felt like eternity. Finally her voice came through the speaker.

"I feel the same way. All right. I'll come to Swiftwater. We still have matters to talk about ..."

Always the analytical one, she let that reminder dangle before finishing in a husky whisper.

"'Til then, and I love you."

He had less than a minute to bask in those final words, folding the sound of Olga's voice into the sight of bright flowers circling the park's flagpole. His buzzing cellphone snapped him back from reverie, and he half expected to hear Olga's voice again. But it was Jason Ferris.

"I'll talk. But only to you. Understood? No gun, no cuffs, and no wire. I'll check before I open my mouth."

Greg was okay on the wire part, but to meet anyone without his gun and cuffs would a serious violation of regulations. Still, it was worth the chance.

"Agreed. Where?"

"That small path off the Old Rail Trail, just past the bridge. You know it?"

It was a good choice. Jason could park at a secluded spot where a byroad met the side trail. Greg could leave his own car near the outdoor railroad museum and come at Jason from the opposite direction.

"Yes. When?"

"Now."

Minutes later, he parked his police car, locked his gun and cuffs in the trunk, and walked a short distance on the Old Rail Trail, then turned left on the smaller path. Initially he passed through a stand of trees, then through the middle of a three- or four-acre cleared area that had once been in cultivation. Now it was covered with calf-high wild grass, changing its color from green to brown.

Jason stood just inside the trees on the other side of the clearing. His car was probably parked farther on, along a seldom-traveled secondary road. Without a word, Jason pantomimed Greg through opening his shirt, raising his trouser legs and turning slowly in a circle. When he finished the routine, Jason walked closer until only five or six paces separated them, then spoke.

"Five minutes."

Greg could see that from where he stood Jason had a view of the clearing, and mostly that's what he kept his eyes trained on. Greg took the initiative.

"Your meeting. Start with why."

"I was set up. But maybe it wasn't you that did it."

"It wasn't."

"I'm not all the way there, but I was pretty sure when I saw McHugh go right to my garage."

A pause. Jason finally looked at him.

"I'm about to take a chance."

"Your choice."

Jason's eyes glowed with intensity.

"I want out, and the police off my back."

"Lots of people want that."

Jason flared.

"Cut the crap. I know you're following procedure. Stick with that, and we get nowhere."

Greg shifted to a deliberately less official tone.

"Tell me exactly what you want. I can't make any promises until you get to specifics."

"McHugh planted evidence in my car. That's why he went straight for the garage. But he didn't find anything there. I have it with me."

"And? What would I do with it?"

"Have someone look at it. No one would have gone to the trouble of planting something unless it tied me to the murder. Only way that could happen is that it's part of other evidence you already have. Maybe taken from the evidence safe."

Greg wouldn't say so, but that thought made a whole lot of sense. Besides, McHugh's tunnel vision made it probable.

"Okay, let's say I do that. Then what?"

"Then you see to it that I'm taken off the suspect list."

"Nice try. But you don't know how things work. This isn't my case. I can't 'see to' anything. Best I could do is take my views to the lead investigator, Espy, who might or might not listen to me in preference to another officer working with him."

"McHugh."

"Yeah. I can only promise that if I find something out of the ordinary, I'll do my best to see that it gets addressed."

Jason remained completely still. After what seemed a long time, he shook himself and walked away a few paces, then back. He pulled a plastic baggie from his pocket and held it up. Inside were what looked like light brown crumbs.

"From my car's glove compartment."

Greg knew this was a moment of truth. A red flag went up, annealed in the historical distrust that Ukrainians had built up about strangers, and reinforced by warnings heard at the police academy. Deals with criminals were dangerous, and could quickly morph into the slippery slope to corruption.

On the other hand, another part of his instinct, impelled by the emphasis on redemption in his Pentecostal faith, announced that before him stood a mortal struggling with good and evil, and seeking a path to the good side.

Not to mention that, as a source, Jason could be crucial.

"Let's say I get you taken off the suspect list. The police still have to find the murderer. We've got to look at a trade here. If you get help, so should we. You've got information or at least access to sources of information that we need."

"I won't be your snitch."

"Not snitching. Just using your computers for… research. We don't have anyone who can dig as deep as you can as fast as you can."

Jason made an angry gesture.

"My computers? At home? I can't go home."

He watched Jason will himself back to calmness.

"Okay, so I can't sit at my computers, but I can still access them. *If* I decide that I want to. Don't forget: it all depends what you've got to offer."

Greg nodded, and laid out the deal.

Jason stood motionless for half a minute more, then did an about face and disappeared into the trees.

4:30 PM

Calla stood in the entrance to Phil's kitchen. For the first time in several days, she felt as if a heavy pack had been lifted off her shoulders. Phil's place exuded the pleasure of well-worn, comfortable clothing. Yet it was unfamiliar enough to give her distance from Swiftwater, the jail, and her clients, even though she could have seen parts of the town down the hill if she'd wanted to.

She managed to put aside the fact that Lonny's freedom was only temporary. It was enough to enjoy the sight of him in a comfortable chair with light coming in from open windows and pleasant views of trees beyond them. The beauty of the room helped, too: old furniture, reflecting the care that went into its creation, each piece with a deep, glowing patina, freshly polished.

Being temporarily free of her worst worries allowed her, finally, to think about other things. Like Phil: how solicitous he was, offering support beyond what even her few close friends had shown when word spread of Lonny's arrest. Here, in his own place, she realized how often thoughts about him had popped up over the last two days.

Lonny slumped in an upright wooden rocker, his dark clothes interrupting the cheerful floral design on the cushions. Calla had expected him to be happier at his release. But outside the police station, his expression, stuck between defeat and sullen anger, was not much different from the look he'd worn inside his cell. He muttered thanks, and, when pressed, said he felt better after his release. But the comment sounded forced.

Close to Lonny, Janice Casey leaned her weak side into the generous arm rest of a sofa covered in the same material as the rocker where Lonny sat. A cup of herbal tea sat half full on the low maple coffee table in front of her. Every time Calla glanced her way, she saw Janice's gaze firmly fixed on Lonny.

Phil had spent the last half hour making people comfortable, moving in and out of the kitchen, preparing tea, a sandwich for Lonny, and offering homemade bread to Janice and to her. Now she heard his whispered voice at her ear.

"It doesn't look as if we'd be missed much if we sat outside for a bit."

She turned her head and found his face close to hers. Only a few inches closer and her cheek would have been on his. She gave a prim nod and a weak smile, hiding the hungry grin that suddenly wanted out.

"I'll let Lonny know."

Lonny's expression didn't change when she said she and Phil were going to sit outside. Both Lonny and Janice indicated wordlessly that they would rather remain indoors.

On the north side of the house, Phil showed her a semicircular patch of tended grass with a planted border. She noticed that he had chosen a mix of local annuals and perennials, not as showy as imported decorations, but more at home. The north side was a good choice, shaded from southern sun when the days grew hotter. Phil sat in a sturdy redwood glider with cushions. There were two matching side chairs. She ignored the chairs and sat beside him.

His hands clasped, unclasped, and clasped again in his lap.

"I guess we shouldn't stay too long. But anyway, we can see the cars and the front and back entrances from here."

The time was theirs, brief as it was. But where to start? She settled on the tried and, sometimes, true.

"Tell me more about yourself."

He laughed.

"The long or short version?"

"You already gave me the short one. Tell me more about your wife."

"Aah. The other woman part."

She wondered if she'd said the wrong thing. Phil must have read her expression. He burst out laughing.

"Just kidding. But I was also thinking how Jean would have reacted to that question. She had a great attitude toward life, and an unbeatable sense of humor. She found the beautiful furniture I've had trouble leaving. She outfitted the kitchen and got me interested in cooking. There were serious times, of course. Learning that she—meaning we—couldn't have children was a heavy one. Worse, I think, for her than the cancer."

He looked upward, his head back and eyelids half-lowered

"She was my perfect match. I loved her deeply. I thought I would die when she died. I grieved for months that turned into years. I found diversions, but nothing like the abiding pleasure I had with Jean. Until now."

He looked at her then, his eyes wide open, but worried.

"This is going fast, maybe too fast. But you asked."

"About Jean?"

"No. About the way I feel about you."

She grabbed his closest hand with both of hers.

"Oh, God, Phil, yes! That's been on my mind, too. Was I that obvious? Wait for me just a second. I don't want my mind on anything else. Let me make sure everything's all right inside and I'll be back."

She almost ran to the house, stepped quickly into the kitchen, and loudly filled two glasses with water. Janice now sat in an arm chair from the dining table, pulled up close to Lonny. His expression combined concentration with something that looked to Calla like relaxation. For a moment she felt a twinge of jealousy, but replaced it right away with satisfaction that Lonny and Janice were getting along so well.

She picked up the water glasses and hurried back to Phil. Standing in front of him, she found no place to put them, except on the ground. She laid them down carefully and sat again, right up next to him. He took her hand immediately and she edged closer, leaning her body against his. Her heart was pounding like a teenager's. She hoped his was doing the same.

His breathing, getting in the way of his words, expressed her feelings as well as his own.

"I wish we were somewhere else. But we aren't."

She nuzzled him and nodded, content just to be close to him for now. They settled for snuggling and quietly exchanging words that jumped forward and back, lightly touching time and feelings. Everything was incomplete, like an outline of things they were agreeing to talk about later. They soon had a rhythm of speaking and listening that she, for all her checkered history of occasional relationships, had never had with anyone else. She had no idea how long they talked, only that she wished they never needed to stop.

It took an outside signal to force a pause. Phil's cell phone buzzed.

She was amazed how normal he managed to sound. She understood part of the message from his end of the conversation, and he summarized the rest when he finished.

"They found evidence in the trailer that ties Harland Casey to Thibodeau's death. He's been arrested. Chief Cisek wants me to take Janice back to the trailer, and ask her to stay there until they can interview her."

He paused and she thought a blush passed across his forehead. But it could have been the blurriness of her own vision.

"I guess I better take her now, though that's the last thing I want to do."

She tried to join his earnest tone.

"That's all right. I ought to be taking Lonny home."

They held hands on the way to the door—like prom dates, she laughed to herself. Phil gave her a warm peck on the cheek. Then they put on their serious faces and walked into the house.

The first thing she noticed was a breeze from an open window, then the absence of conversation. But she wasn't ready for the sight of Janice Casey, a dish towel gagging her mouth and both arms bound to her chair with her dress sash. There was no trace of Lonny. She stood immobilized while Phil went to Janice. An old, sinking feeling started with her hands and feet and sped up its inexorable path to her heart.

As soon as Phil removed the gag and began undoing her arms, Janice started talking.

"I should have called out, but it happened so fast. We were just chatting and all of a sudden he jumped up and grabbed me. I was just too weak to fight him off. I'm sorry. So sorry."

Janice was shaking, tears welling.

Calla pulled herself together enough to go to Janice's side and hold her. The frail body felt like only bone and sinew as Janice began to shake violently.

Phil, near a window, was already on the phone.

"I'd say a half hour, tops. But you know this place sits right at the edge of town. Best guess, he went up toward the ridge where trails branch out in all directions. I'm sorry, Tom. I really messed this one up."

After a pause, Phil's voice went on.

"Sure. I understand. I'll wait here until the officer arrives to take Mrs. Casey back to her trailer… I'm not sure. It's up to Calla whether she goes along."

Phil flashed her the question with his eyes. A sense of duty prodded her to nod an automatic confirmation.

"She's indicating yes… Yeah, I'll come in after that so we can talk."

Lonny was heading up and away. She was in a familiar downward spiral. The last few minutes with Phil had lifted her so high; she didn't know how she'd survive the inevitable crash at the bottom.

And it was all her fault.

4:49 PM

Jason found a corner seat at the computer table in the Esterhill library. In the late afternoon, high school students and the pale, hunched types who haunted libraries filled all the other chairs. It took only a couple of minutes to verify what he'd suspected: the library computers were rigged to block internet downloads. He could get around that problem without too much trouble; he had his iPad, and that would work.

Having to make any kind of a deal with Takarchuk still bothered him. He'd survived as long as he had by building a system that depended entirely on himself. Takarchuk was both a total unknown and a cop. Under any other circumstances, Jason would never have considered making a deal; but circumstances had changed.

One thing was in Takarchuk's favor: he seemed pretty smart. The deal he'd laid out wasn't too far from what Jason might have designed himself. The cop wanted half of the crumbs from Jason's glove compartment. Jason would hold on to the rest. Takarchuk would try a back door to analyze the chemical makeup of the crumbs. What happened next would depend on those results. They could lead to Jason getting off the hook, free to build a new life. Or they could make things worse. That was the kicker.

Meanwhile, he had to hold up one other part of the bargain. Takarchuk wanted more information on Harland Casey. If Jason could tie Casey to Salvation, he could give Takarchuk a leg up within the police department; and that advantage, if the cop did what he said he would, could get McHugh off Jason's back. Too many "ifs", but they were all he had for now.

While he thought, he moved to an upholstered chair in the corner of the library and used the wi-fi signal of the coffee shop two doors down the block to log into his computers remotely.

Soon he was well into the easiest tasks in a process that would get longer and more complicated the deeper he tunneled into it. A general search produced fourteen Harland Caseys in various parts of the United States. Those might be discrete persons, or some could be old shadows of the Harland Casey here in the Cascades as he moved around the country. Before long, he had the Social Security number of the Casey who had spent the most time recently in Arizona. With that in hand, he unearthed a credit card number and a bank account in a regional bank outside Tucson.

Takarchuk had told him that Casey had once done jail time. So he used back doors into national criminal registries, and found that the Harland Casey he was looking at was a registered child sex offender. Specifically, he had served two years in a federal penitentiary, starting in 1985, for a month-long spree with a fifteen-year-old girl. He was then thirty-two at the time. When they were captured, both Casey and the girl had maintained that she went with him voluntarily. Kidnapping and more serious rape charges were dropped, but Casey still was convicted of violation of the Mann Act, transporting a minor across state lines for sexual purposes.

Once out of jail, he drifted. Brief traces of him showed up over an eight-year period in Tennessee, Oklahoma, South Dakota, Montana, and Eastern Washington. He appeared to settle in Arizona about twelve years ago, and the drifting stopped until four years ago when a regular pattern of travel emerged: winters in Arizona and summers in the Northwest. Starting three years after Casey settled in Arizona, the name "Janice Casey" appeared on a joint bank account and other documents.

That was all useful information and he was making progress, but the iPad was cumbersome. To go much further, he'd need to be at his home computers. Besides, working in such a public place made him nervous. As he slung his knapsack over his shoulder, he knew he had discovered at least one thing of importance: Harland Casey was not a central figure in the drug scene. A courier or transporter, maybe, but not a designer and probably not a major buyer or distributor.

Takarchuk had been cagey about why he wanted background on Casey, but a possible reason was emerging. Neither Lonny Ogden nor the guy they called Gabby had the brains or the connections to get their hands on quantities of Salvation and set up a distribution stream. At most they could be mules. Casey, with his annual movement around Washington State and his connections to Arizona, could be important in a regional operation. But someone else was developing the drugs, supplying Casey and directing his schedule.

Jason's concern wasn't Casey's guilt or innocence. Casey was important only if Takarchuk could prove he had a motive to order or carry out Rolf's murder. If Casey was implicated, then Jason would move off the suspect list. But with Casey looking unlikely for the crime, he, Jason, was still in the spotlight.

He'd gotten all the information he could get today, and would report what he'd learned to Takarchuk. Now he had to dig up more data if he wanted to help himself. And to do that, he had to get back home.

6:46 PM

Greg found McHugh at a bar often frequented by cops and firemen on the main road out of Esterhill. The Haymow was simply a hangout. No music, no flickering beer signs, just a metal and fake-stone bar with high-backed swivel stools, booths along one wall, and a few tables. It was a place to sit without distractions in the company of people you could trust. If you happened to mention a case in progress or voice an opinion you didn't want made public, you had no worries. At the Haymow, like in Vegas, what happened there, stayed there.

Greg had been there only once before. The Haymow was a good half hour from Swiftwater, and he grew up with Ukrainians who drank with close friends, usually at their homes. Bars in general were not places where he hung out.

McHugh was at the bar, empty stools on both sides. Greg didn't want to start a serious discussion where others could move in close, nor did he want to make a show of bringing McHugh to an empty booth. Instead, he sat in a booth that was on the way to the men's room and sipped a beer.

He had to wait half an hour until McHugh stood up and walked through the door marked "Guys". When McHugh passed the booth was on his way back to the bar, he called out.

"Hey, Bill. Want to join me?"

McHugh eyed him coolly.

"Not particularly, unless you got something you want to talk about."

"Yes, I do."

For a moment, he thought McHugh would blow him off. But McHugh slowly walked to the bar, got his half-full glass and slid into the opposite seat.

"This couldn't wait 'til we were in the station?"

"It would be better here."

"I suppose I'll find out why."

McHugh's sarcasm and indifference were on full display.

This was the moment. Greg reached into his pocket, placed the baggie with the crumbs from Jason's car in the space between them, and waited.

McHugh flicked the bag.

"What's this?"

"You already know."

McHugh gave no physical reaction.

"No, I don't. Why don't you tell me what I know?"

He took a chance.

"You expected to find these crumbs in Ferris' car when you went to his house this afternoon. You knew they'd be there because you put them there."

McHugh's eyes blazed. Otherwise, he still clung to a cool front.

"That's a serious charge, with no proof."

"It's not a charge. That would be a departmental matter. I just want you to know that I know."

"And why would that be?"

"I've got reason to think Ferris is not the one to like for Rolf's murder. We'd get a lot further in solving it if we were working on the same case."

McHugh dropped his pretense of calm.

"Listen up, shitface. There's no 'together' here. This is a county case. You're just helping out. In fact, you're hindering. I don't need a lecture any more than I need help. When you get as much experience as I have, you'll know what I'm talking about. Until then, shut the fuck up."

McHugh's voice had risen to the point where several heads turned their way. Just as quickly, they turned back, erasing everything they'd heard.

Greg showed no reaction. In the good old USSR, you got a lot of early practice in doing that. His only movement was to slide his hand forward and pull the baggie to his side of the table.

"Just so we're straight, Ferris kept some of these crumbs and his car's glove compartment will still have traces. I haven't done anything with these, but if they get analyzed, I bet they'll match the crumbs in the evidence safe that were found on Rolf's body. That can't be a coincidence. The Sherriff won't think it is."

McHugh tamped his voice down, but his growled whisper carried a louder threat.

"You got no idea what you're messing with, fuckhead, protecting and abetting one of the biggest felons around. You're going down."

"Alleged felon. No convictions. And planting evidence is a felony too."

"He's guilty. Your bleeding heart can't see that. But he'll get you next. That's a promise."

"Maybe. But I don't think so. You know about Harland Casey?"

"So what? More than one person could be involved, but Ferris is behind it all. Always has been."

"You may be right about the past. I'm only saying that I don't think Ferris is good for Rolf's murder. Or Thibodeau's. I got some ideas. But like I said, I'd rather be working together than working against each other."

"Live with it."

Greg stuffed the baggie into his pocket and left the Haymow. Eyes followed him, then blinked his presence away.

7:00 PM

"Didn't I say something about not getting involved? We make some progress and it's matched with more trouble. We make progress on Casey as a suspect, and Lonny Ogden gets away as soon as he makes bail."

The Chief was mad and he had a right to be.

Phil had gone straight to Tom Cisek's office as soon as an officer had driven off with Janice Casey.

"Like I said on the phone, Tom. I screwed up. I should have kept a better eye on Lonny. Believe me, I'm sorry and I'll do whatever I can to get things back on track."

"Now you understand. Why not when it could have made a difference?"

Cisek glowered, threw up his hands and added a muttered answer to his own question.

"Probably had your eye on his sister."

"Is that what it's all about?"

"Naw. Ogden's flight is what matters, and convicting a murderer. But your distraction makes my job harder. It's a small town and word gets around. Some people probably'll think your pecker got in the way of your brain."

Much as it made him wince, Phil knew that assessment was accurate.

"I get you. So where do we go from here? How can I help?"

Tom lightened up a bit.

"Not like you have done. You finally get what I mean? Just let us all do our job. But if you happen to hear of Lonny's whereabouts, you let us know right away."

"That I can do."

"You sure?"

A narrowed look sharpened the question.

"I said I would."

"Good enough. We're copasetic."

"Anything more I need to know about Casey and his status?"

"Not for now, but I'll let you know as usual, Mr. Mayor."

Phil caught the signal that things were creeping back to normal. Or at least as close to normal as circumstances allowed. He would be in the way if he hung around, so he got a cup of coffee at a local roaster, checked his office to make sure nothing else had popped up, and drove to the hatchery to pick up Calla.

She was standing by herself on the big lawn, half in waning sunlight; she climbed into his car with a neutral greeting. Once they were moving, she answered his question about Janice in the way he imagined she reported to her supervisor about the current condition of a client. He heard himself telling her about his conversation with Tom Cisek in the same distracted voice he used with his secretary when too much was on his mind.

He didn't know about Calla, but he wanted a return to the carefree intimacy they had discovered less than two hours ago. That possibility felt both as close as she was beside him, and as far away as the mountain peaks through his windshield. Though she was looking in the same direction, he couldn't tell whether she saw the same mountains or was trapped in other visions that blocked the view.

When they reached the parking lot behind City Hall, Calla's was the only car there. He walked her to it and courteously opened the door. She didn't get in. Instead, she dropped her purse and he saw the desperation on her face. She threw her arms around his neck. Her breath against his ear was warm and real and right, but her voice was anguished, shaky.

"I'm so scared."

His arms went around her. His words emerged in a croak.

"Don't worry. We'll find Lonny."

She didn't move.

"When he runs, there's no finding him. He'll call when he wants to. I'll leave my cell on."

He hugged her tighter, then let go.

"Follow me home."

They prepared food, talking in short bursts, avoiding mention and—as much as possible—thoughts about Lonny. They ate, watched the sun set, suggested music each of them enjoyed, and exchanged smiles when their choices agreed.

But as the evening wore on and bedtime faced them, a different mood descended. He knew what was happening to him and thought he saw the same change in Calla. Their joy in discovering each other had been real, but right now they couldn't sustain it. For each smile and laugh he got out of Calla, he saw, right after it faded, a furtive, far-away look she tried to hide. In conversation lulls, he heard her almost imperceptible sighs.

So he put towels and spare pajamas at the foot of the bed in the guest room, and instructed Calla on the idiosyncrasies of a hot water faucet he hadn't gotten around to fixing. She nodded her understanding and, if it wasn't just his imagination, her relief.

He hugged her, held a lingering kiss on her forehead and retreated to his own bed, where sleep would not come. After what seemed like hours, the door creaked open and he felt her warm body beside him. She snuggled against him, and soon he heard her breathing lengthen and grow regular.

He luxuriated in the sensation of her nearness until sleep erased any further thoughts.

9:35 pm

Jason drove to Lila's place. He'd called her at work, told her to plead sickness and meet him right away. She hadn't protested at all.

When he entered the house she was already there, and he wasted no time on greetings.

"Lila, the time has come. We need to get out of here right now. Start something new. I have a place in Montana where all of us can stay. But if we don't go right now, we may not get another chance."

As he spoke, he opened a canvas briefcase and showed her the banded $10s and $20s; $10,000 in all.

"I have more of these, Lila. A lot more. Enough for all of us to be safe and free."

She only glanced at the money, then directly at him, hope rising, retreating, and finally finding a permanent place in her eyes. From that moment on, everything went quickly.

Lila retrieved a large, worn duffle bag and wordlessly went from closet to closet, grabbing clothes. He wondered how many times she had had to do exactly that before. A cardboard box was soon filled with Jace's toys, and a second box with food. Fifteen minutes after Lila started, they were ready to go. She walked out the door, carrying Jace, without another glance around her. This place, like many others Jason could only imagine, was done with.

In that moment, as Lila walked toward the car, he realized how much his own hope rose with her willingness to depend on him. And that he was actually accepting responsibility for another person in the way he'd promised himself he would never do. Up to this moment he had thought of possibilities; now he was making them real. He felt giddiness, and a little fear. Fear not for himself, but for these two beings who would, from now on, depend on him.

On the nearly deserted interstate, they made it to his cabin in Montana's Bitterroot Mountains in less than five hours. Jace slept and Lila dozed most of the way. As they approached their destination, he told Lila all she needed to know about the small town ten miles away, the location of the closest market and the medical clinic.

Just before 3:00 am, they arrived. He used a flashlight to show Lila the garage with the pick-up truck and his gleaming black motorcycle. Before handing her keys to the house, he explained the complex alarm system and the satellite connection to his computers in Portal.

Casual thieves would be deterred by the house's heavy oak doors and window shutters. More serious burglars would have to contend with the most ear-splitting claxons and sirens available. A huge propane tank behind the garage and the industrial-size generator that ran off of it would give her electricity for several weeks, enough time for him to return and arrange for the tank to be refilled.

He got ready for the drive back, while Lila stood quietly to one side. When he opened the car door, she all but ran to him. She threw her arms over his neck, her head down on his chest. He barely heard her; but, as he drove off, her words filled his ears and, as he realized, his heart, cancelling all other sounds.

"When we were little, I believed you were my only protector. Then I stopped believing it. Now it's true."

DAY FOUR

Calla entered her apartment as if it were an alien starship. Could it have been just a few days ago that this space had been familiar—a modest, yet adequate expression of her style and her life? Now her heart was filled with the sights and smells of a different place, of comfortable old furniture pieces, of Phil among them.

She had come back to consciousness beside Phil at sunrise, feeling like a beautiful flower opening to the light. For a while, the rest of the world didn't exist. They held each other and savored the moment. When her feet were back on the floor, she went on feeling as refreshed and rested as if she had been on vacation.

Full of that delight, she had driven right away to the hatchery to check on Janice. No one had asked her to do so, but professional habit and personal compassion took her there. She'd arrived at the trailer just after 7:30 am. Despite the fact that Janice had said she always rose early, Calla hesitated to disturb her at that hour. But she'd knocked anyway. There was no response. And none to a second try. She was turning away when the door opened.

Janice glared with a severity that surprised her. Was she showing anger over Lonny's aggression, or was she making disapproving assumptions about a social worker who was wearing the same clothes she'd worn the evening before? Janice was fully dressed, in pants and a sturdy shirt, her hair pinned into a bun. Though she still leaned on her crutch, she appeared more erect than usual. He voice was level, though challenging.

"What do you want?"

"Good morning, Janice. To see if you're okay."

"You can take me off your list. I'm fine."

"Sure you don't need anything?"

Real anger had reached Janice's eyes, matching lips that twisted almost into a snarl.

"Maybe you're getting deaf. Nothing! I've been on my own most of my life and can do just fine without Harland. The stupid fool."

Calla offered, in return, the only thing she could.

"Let me know if you change your mind."

The door was already closing when Janice's parting words reached her.

"I won't."

Remembering the visceral impact of those words brought Calla back to where she stood in her apartment. They also prompted her first focused thoughts about Lonny since she had left Phil. With a free half-hour before she needed to leave for her first appointment, she decided to have another look at the few belongings Lonny kept there. There was no real hope, she told herself, that anything she found would give her a clue to Lonny's whereabouts; but looking would at least keep her occupied.

In her spare room, a home-office desk sat across from the foldout couch where Lonny slept during his infrequent visits. A high shelf in the closet held a sleeping bag, a pillow, and clean towels. Beside them was a battered supermarket bag. Calla wasn't sure when Lonny had brought that in.

The first item in the bag was a shirt that needed laundering. She threw it on the floor to wash later. A belt and an older portable am/fm radio were next. Two well-thumbed fantasy comic books were the only other visible items. Idly, Calla lifted one of them to get a closer look, and a glint caught her eye.

Between the comic books was an amulet, with colored beads and small stones mounted around the outer edge of an oblong copper disk about three inches long. Etched lines suggested mountains behind three stick trees, near which a snake was coiled. A leather thong, tied to form a circle, ran through a clasp at the top of the amulet.

She was stunned. The amulet released an immediate flashback. She pictured it hanging around a man's neck, so close that she could make out details in the scene, especially the snake. The man wearing the amulet was her mother's live-in boyfriend, Sven Carlson, a person Calla had initially liked, then distrusted and ultimately detested. In this memory, her mother was out and she was alone with the large, unkempt male making a move on her. He was also half-drunk, and that saved her. She feinted one way and ducked under his arm the other. In the moment she slipped away from his grasp, the amulet was in the middle of her vision, imprinted on her memory.

Sven was twenty years older than her mother: a drifter, but also a charmer. She had been twelve when he moved in, fourteen when Lonny was born and she moved away to live with relatives for three years. Sven was Lonny's father; he hung around for just a few years after Lonny arrived. When he left, with her mother going downhill, Calla had moved back and, without realizing it, began her lifelong care of Lonny.

She didn't remember much about Sven. He'd introduced her mother to daily drinking, turning her into an alcoholic who had permanently damaged Lonny in the womb. He beat her mother from time to time, and would have beaten her, too, except that she found ways to hide or get out of the house when he started drinking. He was dark-haired like some other Swedes she had met, and had light blue-grey eyes. Lonny's eyes. He liked to boast of his white family's frontier exploits in Montana; but when he got drunk enough, he'd tell stories about the years he spent on the Pitpit reservation, befriended by a native family. Then his speech dropped into a sing-song intonation.

Sven was never without his amulet. She had more than once seen him get out of the shower, a towel around his waist and the amulet around his neck. So how did the amulet get into this box in her house? Lonny had been too young to know his father. When Sven left, he left for good. He never made any effort to find out about his son, much less to contact him. She had no idea what had happened to Sven, except for hearing once, in passing, that someone by that name had died in an accident in the late 1990s.

She hated the amulet because of the man who'd worn it. But it was the only possible clue she had to Lonny's whereabouts. With reluctance, she wrapped the amulet in a washcloth and shoved the bundle into the bottom of her purse.

Fifteen minutes later she was listening to the story of a forlorn widow whose only son was out of work and could no longer send her money. Social Security was not enough for her basic needs; the gas and electric companies were threatening to cut off service. Calla took notes and promised to try to call off the utility companies. There was a chance she could get the woman into an emergency food stamp program; the widow had already used up her full allotment of regular assistance. Beyond that, there was not much the county could do.

As she listened, she worried that she was not really serving the people who needed her. On auto-pilot, she wasn't conscious enough to look deep and identify underlying problems. She pushed guilt aside with the simple, cool recognition that her reality was what it was. Self-flagellation would change nothing.

And there was another part of that reality. Something that had been missing before. She recognized a strengthening will to fight back harder against her worries. She could see a glimpse of happiness in her budding relationship with Phil, and unaccustomed laughter was finding its way into her throat. How good, and how overdue, those fresh feelings felt!

She wasn't about to let worry and the specter of a tiny old amulet carry her back to a perpetual state where everything—her circumstances, Lonny, the world itself—was ominous and hopeless.

Not this time.

The new feelings lasted a few minutes. Long enough for her to know that they were real and that, even as they faded, she could get them back. They were getting stronger, but they weren't strong enough to blot out completely the undeniable fact that Lonny was gone.

And he still had to be found.

10:30 AM

Greg sat in the corner of the interview room at the sheriff's office in Esterhill. Espy and McHugh, as the principals in the case, occupied chairs at a steel table with Harland Casey opposite them. At Casey's left sat Alice Downey, a public defender who late yesterday had been assigned as Casey's counsel. Apparently listening with one ear, she studied the documents she'd been given only this morning.

Espy, as lead investigator, asked most of the questions.

"Let's start over. We have your fingerprint on a syringe we found in the trailer. The syringe contained traces of the poison that killed Thibodeau. How did your print get there?"

Alice Downey looked up; the room was treated to piercing cornflower eyes under a blonde bob. With her gray suit and leather briefcase, she was the most formal item in the room.

"He doesn't have to answer that."

Espy replied evenly.

"We've been here for an hour and your client has answered zero questions. He can do what he wants, of course, but if he carries that attitude to trial, the jury will look at evidence and he'll go down."

Downey waived an impatient hand.

"So what have you got? Proximity, the syringe? That's it? No motive. The tox results show a drug cocktail and a poison. My client might have injected the victim with a substance that was presumed by both parties to be a beneficial drug. You might cook up a minor felony out of that, but not manslaughter and certainly not murder. You're looking for a confession that will save you from having to prove your case. That's not going to happen. Reduce the charge to something reasonable and we can talk. Otherwise, let's wrap this up."

Espy sat back, holding his pen up toward his shoulder. He looked at McHugh and got a head shake.

"Officer Takarchuk, any questions occur to you?"

A question *had* been building, made up mostly of a string of inconsistencies in Harland's character. Proof or no proof, there was nothing about him that added up to Casey being an organized crook, much less a murderer. He could be a skilled actor. But even that possibility seemed like a stretch.

"Who are you covering up for, Mr. Casey?"

Casey's head was down when Greg asked the question, and he kept it down. As if to accentuate the fact that his silence was intentional, Casey finally looked up and locked eyes with Greg for a moment before settling into a blank stare at the wall off to the side.

Greg tried one more tack.

"Could you tell me your wife's maiden name?"

Silence again.

Alice Downey looked at him.

"Relevance?"

He was thinking about how to respond when Espy decided for him.

"This interview is over. Thank you for time Mr. Casey, Ms. Downey. We may resume this interview at a later time."

Downey was the first up. Espy collected his papers and walked into the outer office. Greg and McHugh started to leave when suddenly Casey spoke. He was facing his counsel and shaking his head, but he could have been addressing anyone in the room.

"Lowry. She was Janice Lowry. All these brains here in this room, and still not a clue."

An officer came in and walked Casey back to his cell, his shackles echoing down the corridor as he walked. Downey followed him, but her attention was more on her phone than her client. McHugh stuck his head back into the interrogation room and called out.

"So you got your answer but so what? Not significant to the investigation."

Greg dug in.

"I don't think he did it, killed Thibodeau on his own."

"So you're smarter than the rest of us."

"Got nothing to do with smarts. Just that maybe we haven't looked at the situation in the right way."

"And what, in your opinion, would be the right way?"

For the first time, he heard an undertone of interest compete with McHugh's usual aggressiveness.

"We haven't checked out the wife."

McHugh scoffed.

"The cripple? Yeah, she's a likely murderer."

"Likely? I don't know. But that's the point. We know nothing about her. We've treated her as a weak partner. Maybe she's not so weak."

McHugh shrugged.

"In a perfect world we would have enough resources to investigate every person at the hatchery. But we don't."

Silence. Greg broke it only after steeling himself against McHugh's inevitable reaction.

"You're right. We don't have the resources to investigate Janice Casey. But I think I know who might help us."

McHugh stiffened and so did his voice.

"If you know where fuckhead Ferris is, you better give him up. He's still officially a suspect."

"You don't have to keep telling me about your opinion of the guy. I get it. But he might be able to help us get a leg up on this case. I don't know where Ferris is, but I think I can contact him."

Outwardly, McHugh was still deep in his critical, stubborn position. But in his parting words, Greg could hear the echo of new interest.

"What the fuck, do what you want. My warning about Ferris still stands and you'll find out soon enough why. While you're doing that, I'll see if Espy wants a look at Mrs. Casey."

11:05 AM

Jason parked on the slope that rose up to form the ridge behind Portal. He was at the edge of the town's dwellings and could see most of the houses, including his own.

He should have felt more tired than he did. Thirty-six hours without sleep and he hadn't crashed. It was like old times, when he pulled two and three all-nighters routinely. Only this wasn't old times. He didn't know what to call it. "New times" sounded made up. And he still didn't have anything solid that he could count on. But he'd *done* something.

Besides, for the first time he could remember, he had done something impulsively. Impulse was another word for danger in the drug business, and ran counter to the careful, constantly-monitored life he'd built. Taking Lila and Jace away was a real break with his past.

Gazing down on Portal, he realized that if he was serious about protecting his new—the word felt strange—*family*, he had to finish what he started here. Otherwise the police might go on looking for him; and if they looked hard enough, they would find him. Finishing meant doing what he promised Takarchuk, which required getting back to his computers. But could he risk it? Was his place still being watched, and was McHugh setting a trap?

He called Takarchuk.

"Where are you, Jason?"

"Around. Close enough. That information you wanted? Got some, but can't get any more without my computers."

"I talked to McHugh. He didn't exactly admit he tried to set you up. Didn't deny it either. He won't make a move on you if you go home."

"What makes you so sure?"

"The cookie crumbs he put in your glove compartment box him in. At least for now. I haven't told anyone else about them, but McHugh knows I will if I need to. Any other move on you right now will only complicate things for him."

Jason still wasn't sure. The rules were different in this world he'd avoided for so long. But there was no avoiding a choice.

"Okay."

Takarchuk wasn't finished.

"And Jason, when you look, see what you can find on Janice Casey. Or Janice Lowry. That might have been her previous name. She's married now to Harland Casey."

"Any idea where she might have lived when she was young?"

"No."

That would make for a longer search, but not necessarily a dead end. He had started other searches with less to go on. He drove slowly down the slope to the area around his house, circling once in his car and then more carefully on foot until he was sure that no police cars were in the vicinity. Nothing had been disturbed inside his house, and the air felt heavy and unused. He opened several windows and made coffee while he waited for his computers to fire up and complete their security checks.

It was easy to find traces of a Janice Casey going back about ten years in the Tucson area. That would probably coincide with her marriage to Harland. There was nothing unusual in the record: residence for several years in one house off Route 19 halfway to Nogales; joint checking and savings accounts with modest balances; regular payment of all taxes. He found no record of employment for either a Janice or Harland Casey, but, starting with income tax returns, uncovered a yearly income of about forty thousand dollars from interest earned. A deeper look revealed that the interest came from a portfolio of blue-chip stocks and US Treasury and tax-free municipal bonds.

He dug deeper. Now that he had a Social Security number, he found a Marie Casey, and earlier a Marie Lowry, with the same number. Jason made a working assumption that Janice Casey had been Marie Lowry, became Marie Casey when she married Harland, and after that started using Janice as her first name.

Following Marie Lowry, he discovered that she had lived in and around Tucson since the mid-1990s and had been employed by a firm called BosChem Analysts. From the company's web site, he learned that Tom Boswell, a chemist, had founded the company in 1985. It offered chemical analysis services to large industries and mining companies throughout the Southwest.

The BosChem site showed information on its current senior and technical staff but nothing on past employees. Jason figured he had gotten as much information as he could using the anonymity of his computers. The best bet now would be to contact someone at BosChem. Takarchuk might or might not want to do that. But if he didn't, Jason was not about to.

He had stuck his neck out this far. But no farther.

2:16 PM

Phil reflected on the day so far. He'd been up early as usual, and tried to follow his morning routine. But the clear, bright energy of a new day refused to arrive. His heart and mind were bound up with Calla and her distress over Lonny.

Was there anything he could do, he'd asked himself, either as an interested bystander or as Mayor? Truthfully, nothing. Lonny's whereabouts were a matter for the police or the sheriff's deputies. He *wanted* to be able to help the woman that he found himself inescapably attracted to. That attraction had come on strong, but now was stuck up to its axles, spinning its wheels. Not a very romantic metaphor, he thought, but an accurate one.

Throughout the morning he'd suffered through a round of meetings that confirmed the state of the city's finances and the canyon-sized divide among his constituents over what to do about that situation. Still, he knew he had to go through the motions.

He decided to use his lunch hour for a quick visit to the hatchery. Despite dim hope of helping to find Lonny, he was impelled by the need to do something, even if it produced nothing solid. His first stop was with the hatchery manager, who made it quietly clear that, much as he was sorry about Thibodeau's death, the fish were his main concern. Selected male and female salmon were being put in the same tank to spawn, the delicate finale to weeks of computer and behavioral analysis. As Phil left, the manager was already back with the numbers on the paper in front of him.

Next stop was the Casey trailer. It was closed up and quiet except for the hum of an air conditioner. Normal looking. If it were earlier in the day, he would guess that Janice was sleeping in. He mounted the metal stairs to the screen door on the trailer's side and spotted a 3x5 card taped next to the handle. The block letters were emphatic: DO NOT DISTURB. WANT TO BE ALONE.

The pickup normally parked beside the trailer was gone.

It wasn't his job to check further. But even though he shouldn't check, Calla might. She did that kind of thing, and he wanted to hear her voice. He punched in Calla's number.

She answered quickly.

"Phil! What's up?"

"Janice left a note on the trailer, saying she wants no visitors; but the pickup is gone. Maybe she's all right, but there's always the possibility that she isn't. She might be running errands. Thought you might want to check up on her."

"I've got one more person waiting on me, but I can get to the hatchery in about an hour."

She sounded tired. Or was it cautious, reassessing their relationship?

"I'd wait for you if I thought that would help. But I have one more meeting scheduled."

If she said she needed help, he'd find a way to cancel or postpone. "I can manage."

He had no doubt that she could. But he didn't want to end their conversation on such an impersonal note. Especially not now. He hoped he wasn't being too forward as he moved away from the trailer.

"I want to see you soon, if I can."

He waited nervously.

"I want that more than anything, but I'm no good to you until we find Lonny. It's just too hard now."

His heart swooped and spun and couldn't find a landing place. She wanted to be with him! He understood the Lonny part and he ached to hold her, to comfort her. But for her sake, he tried to pretend he was on rock-solid ground.

"We'll do it. We'll find him. Then we'll find out a lot more about each other. Don't worry."

3:05 PM

Greg listened to Jason's report, taking notes, impressed by the organized simplicity with which Jason transmitted the essentials. He also registered the unmistakable message: this is the end. Jason had done what was asked, but don't ask for more.

He looked at his watch, factored in the one hour time difference with Arizona, and reckoned he might still reach someone at BosChem Analysts. When a receptionist answered, he asked to be transferred to the personnel manager, who turned out to be a woman with a crisp style, an accent that he associated with Texans he'd known, and an attitude that announced she was a guardian, not a fount of information.

He was thanking her in advance for the help he hoped she'd provide, when the woman broke in.

"Are you a policeman?"

He stopped for a moment, taken aback.

"Well, yes, I was going to tell you that. How did you guess?"

"Six years as a secretary with the Corpus Christy police."

Her protective responsibility was on full display.

"Well, let's not get too hung up on that, Cassandra—Cassie, is it?

"Casssie's okay. What do you want?"

"Just a confirmation of employment. Can you give me that?"

She paused.

"That much, yes."

"All right, can you confirm that a Marie Lowry was an employee of BosChem from 1986 to 2000."

A computer beeped.

"Yes, that is correct."

"And her job title?"

Initial reluctance in the sound a throat clearing. Then a careful reply.

"Her final title was Research Analyst 1."

"She left in good standing?"

Sternness now, the Texas twang pronounced.

"That would be a matter for senior management. I'll transfer you to our CEO Tom Boswell."

Boswell was no less formal, though willing to provide, in a limited way, additional information about Marie Lowry.

"We were a new, growing company when we decided to hire more chemists. Marie was just finishing a PhD in chemistry at Montana State. We already had one person from that program and were very satisfied with him. She had training in plant chemistry, and we had no one with that background. Turns out that was a good choice, because we eventually got contracts with several big agribusinesses."

"How was she as an employee?"

A chair creaked over the phone and Boswell turned cautious.

"You say you're with the police. Is Marie in some kind of trouble? If she is, and it's serious enough to drag in our name, I'm going to have to stop talking. Why do you want to know about her?"

"I can't get into that kind of detail."

Silence at the other end. Greg tried to help things along.

"Look, Mr. Boswell. I appreciate your position. It's unlikely that there will be blowback for your company. I'm only collecting preliminary information to aid an investigation."

Boswell chose his words carefully.

"I can tell you this much. Marie was bright and competent. Mostly, she wanted to work alone. Had no close friends in the company. Her results were always accurate and on time. In fact, the quality of her work was what allowed us to get agribusiness contracts quicker than we initially expected to."

"Did she give a reason for leaving?"

"No. And there was no question that we would have kept her on. She just walked in one day and gave notice, and didn't want to discuss her reasons."

"As far as you know, did she have any financial problems?"

"I'd say the opposite. We didn't give employees stock options, though we did offer an insider rate if they wanted to buy stock in BosChem. Marie bought more stock than any other employee. She sold her stock in 2001, at a good, though not huge, profit. So I think she was doing all right."

"Anything else you want to add?"

"Unless you are more specific, that's all I'm able to tell you."

He thanked Boswell and hung up.

His first reaction was that Boswell had described a person almost opposite from the Janice Casey he'd met. The woman at the hatchery seemed crippled not just in her body, but by life. That image didn't mesh with a woman who had an advanced education and impressive former career. At the very least, they needed to find out why respected biochemist Marie Lowry had decided to hide her past behind the façade of crippled, dependent Janice Casey.

He called Espy and got McHugh instead. After Greg filled him in, McHugh spoke gruffly, but less antagonistically than before.

"Gotta say that's not bad work. Even if you trusted Ferris more than you should have. We can use the fact that Janice Casey once went by the name Lowry, and that she has a Montana State connection. Our contacts in Bozeman can find out more."

"Should I bring her in?"

"Espy and I will take care of that."

Officially, he had done all that he could do, for now. But he hadn't forgotten about the bartender at the Wayside. He had put off tracking her down because other matters had captured his attention. Now, as the case grew murkier, every new piece of information could be valuable. He'd find the bartender and see what she knew.

4:22 PM

A few tourists wandered on the large hatchery lawn, peering into windows of the buildings; a police car was already parked in the lot when Calla pulled in. A sign on the Visitors' Center door announced that visits were temporarily suspended. No surprise there, what with both the Caseys unavailable, the workload of the hatchery staff at a seasonal high, and the fall-out around Gabby's death.

Her job had required some interaction with the sheriff's office over the years and she remembered having been introduced to Detectives Espy and McHugh before. They were conversing near the Casey trailer as she walked over.

"Is everything all right?"

Espy gave her a quick look.

"Calla Ogden, Lonny's sister, right?"

"Right. County Social Services. I came back out here to check on Janice Casey."

"*Back* out here? You were here before?"

"Early this morning. I talked to Janice and she said she wanted to be left alone for a while. By now I thought she might be willing to talk."

Espy and McHugh traded looks. McHugh took over.

"We got here a little while ago. Mrs. Casey's gone. She give you any indication she wanted to go somewhere?"

Calla now realized that the pickup that usually stood by the trailer was missing.

"No. She was definite about not wanting to be disturbed, and I thought that meant she intended to stay in the trailer."

Espy and McHugh conferred in whispers.

"Okay Ms. Ogden, we'll take it from here. Let us know immediately if Mrs. Casey contacts you or if you hear anything about her you think we need to know."

"You can count on that."

They weren't going to tell her more.

She walked slowly back to her car, some of this morning's heaviness returning. No more client visits were scheduled today, so she had time to herself, meaning, unfortunately, time to feel alone and, if she didn't watch herself, hopeless as well. Her faint hope that Janice might have some idea of Lonny's whereabouts had disappeared with the woman.

She remembered Phil's offer to call at any time. Well, she'd find out if he meant it. She thumbed in his number and he answered immediately in a low voice.

"Calla... you caught me right in the middle of something, but I'll call you back soon. Promise."

Within five minutes he made good on his promise.

"Sorry about that. I was talking with Officer Takarchuk about new information on Janice Casey. No one knows where she is, but some interesting things have come up ..."

Calla's mind wandered away, searching Phil's tone of voice for what it might reveal beyond its crisp professionalism. She returned to what he was saying in the middle of a sentence.

"... and what may be really important is the fact that in addition to being a biochemist for more than ten years, Janice at that time was known by the name Marie."

That name. It was familiar. A former client? Calla's mind flashed momentarily on the old Pitpit Reservation. But that was a place she didn't want to go. It was all she could do to deal with the issues at hand, particularly the ones swirling around Lonny. She willed away memories of a past she wanted to forget and agreed to meet Phil in half an hour.

But as soon as she punched off, the name "Marie" pushed its way back into her thoughts and Calla gave in. She relaxed as she had at Ada's trailer, this time encouraging her mind to settle in that middle space where past and present, facts and fragments of memory, sought common definition.

An image formed of herself as a child, with an older person, someone named Marie—and, to her surprise, that image included the bead and copper amulet. She tried to see more, but her mind wasn't ready to go further, to put those separate elements together. Calla sensed they were part of something larger. In time, they might resolve. Then she would know, but not until then.

She started the car and drove toward Phil, happy with the anticipation of seeing him again. Trying, too—and only partly succeeding—to banish Marie, the amulet, and her childhood to some distant place until she could return to them again.

6:28 PM

At the Wayside Inn, Greg found a female behind the long plank bar and took a seat at the end, away from other customers. The after-work crowd was still around, though some were getting up to leave as he walked in. When the bartender came to take his order, he introduced himself. She waited a moment, sizing him up, before nodding.

"Are you the cop who was asking for me?"

She was in full Goth get-up: short hair dyed coal black, heavy black make-up around dark eyes, and a black sheath dress over calf-length boots. One nostril sported a ring, and a small ball bearing on her tongue came and went as she talked.

"Yes. I want to talk to you about Lonny Ogden. You know him?"

Another studied nod.

"Will this take long?"

Her body language and tone of voice added a languid "whatever".

"It shouldn't."

She walked away without another word and tended to a few things at the other end of the bar, taking her time. Eventually she returned and slouched in front of him again, giving him an opening.

"A couple of evenings ago, you were behind the bar when Lonny came over to talk to a small man seated here."

"I remember."

He got his first close look at her eyes. He saw intelligence behind the façade, and doubted she missed much. His interest in what she could tell him increased.

"Did you hear any of their exchange?"

"No."

"Notice anything unusual about the man with Lonny?"

The look she gave him might have been mockery.

"Only that it wasn't a man."

The statement was like a physical jolt. He tried to tamp down any visible reaction. He needed to be sure.

"What makes you think that?"

"The way she sat. Hands were too small. Used a napkin in a way a man wouldn't. Little things. She was trying hard to look like a man, though."

"Anything else?"

"They knew each other. Lonny kept crowding in close. I've seen him in here a few times. Mostly he stays away from people."

"Did they talk long?"

"Two minutes or so. Then the woman gave something to Lonny. He palmed it and went back to his table, and the woman laid down enough money for a beer—which she hadn't touched—and a tip. Then she left. That's it. You know all I know. Now ..."

She turned away.

"... I've got real customers."

"Just one more thing."

She stopped, looked back without facing him, leaning toward the other end of the bar.

"Did you notice what time Lonny left?"

"12:32."

She must have seen the skepticism on his face, because she went on.

"Exactly then. In the last hour, I count the minutes until I'm outta here. Gets me through to closing."

Greg saw the challenging glint in her eye, but that was enough. Lonny was drugged before he ever left the Wayside, and now a credible witness had him leaving the bar too late to have driven to the crime scene and committed the murder within the coroner's time frame.

Outside, he called Espy's cell. Espy listened and made an immediate assessment.

"Add that to what you told McHugh earlier today, and we've got several reasons to re-interview Harland Casey. He's not been leveling with us. We need to find out why. I'll set it up for first thing tomorrow. Plan to be in Esterhill by 7:30."

DAY FIVE

12:06 AM

Midnight. The start of a new day, a new life. Jason knew the time had come, just as he always figured it would. And when it did—when he finally cut all contact with the drug world—it wouldn't be because he was arrested. It would be because he made the choice.

He was in a relatively safe position with the cops, but he had no illusions that Takarchuk's cooperative attitude would last. Same thing with McHugh, who was temporarily in a box but would be on the attack the second he was sprung loose. This was not just a moment. This was *the* moment.

Jason had never felt more focused and single-minded. He started with the garage. That was easy: the car, which he would take, and a few tools. The rest he could replace. Next, his computers and peripherals: back-up hard drives, top-of-the-line modems and routers, more than 200 feet of Cat 6 cable; they went into custom cases lined with anti-static material. Standard manuals and references could stay where they were.

He hadn't decided whether he would return to internet sales just to have something to do, but he'd have the computers if that's what he chose. Money was no problem, what with twelve online accounts with different banks in different names. Beyond that, he had a large stash of cash buried in three parcels in Montana, used money in small denominations, already sorted by printing dates. He'd spend the oldest money first, never keeping any bills so old that they would attract attention.

For good measure he took out some of the sensors for his home security system. He didn't think anyone could extract information about him from that equipment. But the fact that he had a better security system in place than most banks might be an indication to anyone who stumbled on them that the former occupant of this house had something to hide.

He then filled two heavy-duty leaf bags, one with items he wanted to keep, and the other with things he would dispose of. Some of his clothes, as well as toiletries, went into the "save" bag, along with items from his workroom. He didn't have that many things anyway.

Few had any sentimental value, except for the shirt he was wearing the night he found Lila and Jace. He kept good boots and his warmest clothes. Montana winters could be brutal. In the kitchen he grabbed two small appliances and a set of favorite knives.

The bulging plastic bags went into the back seat of his car; the computer cases were stacked snuggly in the trunk. He got out the Miele vacuum cleaner and went over everything, checking, as he cleaned, for anything he might have missed. When he was finished, he looked around. A first-time visitor would find a neat one-bedroom dwelling with clean, good-quality furnishings and hardwood floors. There was nothing to hint about the former occupant's complicated past.

He wondered idly who would get the place and how soon. He had always left a sizable credit on his utility bills; tomorrow, the post office would receive his order to hold mail until further notice. He hardly got any, as it was. Because he had been so discreet, it might be months before neighbors or some meter reader reported the place empty, and months more before some bureaucrat decided what to do about it. From this moment on, the place was only a collection of stuff. Jason wouldn't miss it. It was already gone.

He locked up the house. A single lamp with an extended-use bulb burned in the living room. It was on a timer that would turn it off later, and on again every evening.

Driving out of Portal at 2 a.m., Jason didn't look back. He remembered some of the words to the song about happiness being "Lubbock in the rear view mirror" and tried humming with "Portal" instead of "Lubbock" in the lyrics. But it didn't work because it didn't matter.

If happiness was anywhere, it was up ahead.

7:56 AM

With Tom Cisek beside him, Phil sat on one of three steel chairs in the dimly-lit observer's space of the Esterhill sheriff's office. The chairs faced a one-way mirror that looked into a bright interrogation room where an officer was moving around, checking recording equipment, placing note pads and bottles of water on a table. Phil could hear his movements through the speaker above the mirror.

He hoped Calla was still asleep, finally getting much-needed rest. He closed his eyes and thought about last evening with her. She'd snuggled into him as she recounted yesterday's events. He couldn't see a direct connection, but somehow those events impelled her to reflect about her life as a girl on the reservation, a man named Sven Carlson, and an old amulet. And about a woman named Marie.

Carlson was the part of the puzzle most familiar to her. But she wasn't able to recall anything more about Marie, other than the vague recollection of a sometime baby sitter. He could feel her tense as she struggled to add more detail to her memory.

Drowsiness had eventually overtaken them. They'd fallen asleep on the couch. When Phil awoke a few hours later, he fetched a blanket for Calla and fell across his bed, fully clothed, out cold until the sun woke him. Two aspirin did little to relieve an insistent headache.

The headache was disappearing when he called Tom. Calla's dim recollections might not add up to much, but the Chief had asked to be informed. Phil pictured Tom mentally hitching up his thoughts as he replied.

"I'm not sure if any of what you say figures in with what we're going to ask Harland Casey in about an hour, but we might hear some things from him that bear on what you and Ms. Ogden were talking about. Never know. Come on in for the first part, if you want to, and figure whether it's worth staying or not."

A sharp scraping sound interrupted his reverie, bringing him back to his chair in the observation area. He looked over at Tom.

"Have a good nap, Phil?"

"Just thinking."

Through the one-way mirror, they watched Harland Casey walk to the chair facing them from the other side of the table. McHugh, Espy, and Takarchuk entered after him and took seats with their backs to the mirror. Harland's face, as he waited in mounting tension, was a constantly changing kaleidoscope of sly detachment, bravado, and bewilderment.

Espy took him through the usual preliminaries, establishing identity, time, and place for the video record and, at the end, asked

Harland if he wanted legal counsel present. Harland made a face and a motion of dismissal.

"Naw. Wouldn't help."

Espy leaned forward and raised his voice a notch.

"Help what, Harland?"

"My situation. The trouble I'm in."

"What trouble would that be?"

Harland fell back on bravado.

"C'mon. It's your case. You make it."

"Actually, Harland, the case is pretty much made. Your prints on the truck keys and the syringe. Together they make you good for both Rolf's and Gabby's murders. That and your refusal to offer any alternate explanation. But we're not here to ask you more about all that right now. We're here for something else."

Harland's eyebrows rose, then his face turned cagey, waiting.

Espy cleared his throat.

"Where was your wife, Janice, on the night of Rolf's murder?"

Harland froze momentarily. He licked his lips.

"At home. With me. Most of the night."

"Most?"

"Well, I don't keep an eye on her all the time, you see. I might go for a walk. She might go for a walk. So I can't say for sure exactly where she was."

"I see. Well, maybe there's something you can say for sure. Why did your wife choose to stop going by the name Marie?"

Harland's expression went blank. Then his face battled conflicting emotions and his breathing turned ragged. His shoulders twitched up and down. Phil imagined his hands clenching and unclenching behind his back.

Espy dropped his pen and put his hand palm down on the table, waiting Casey out. Almost a full minute passed before he spoke again.

"Got nothin' to say about that."

Espy didn't move.

"Harland, you're not helping yourself. We can keep you here as long as we need to, to get at the truth."

"That would be just fine."

In the statement, Phil heard something new, reminding him of a hard-shelled nut cracking.

Espy tried again, raising his hand, palm up.

"If you help us clear you, you'll be out. Otherwise you stay. Which do you want?"

"To stay."

With that admission, Harland's posture straightened and the expression on his face simplified.

"I need protection. From her. From the person you should be talking to."

Espy kept his voice steady and calm.

"Her? Who do you mean, Harland?"

"Janice, my wife. My jailer. The person who can hurt me much more than you can."

"Okay, tell us."

Harland was already talking, words spewing from him in a flood.

"You think of the devil as this big guy with horns and a spear and fire all around him. But the devil I live with is a sneaky-smart woman with a crutch. She can fool anyone. What more do you need to know?"

McHugh spoke up.

"How about drugs?"

Harland nodded.

"Drugs, yeah. I bet she knows more about the chemistry of drugs than anyone. Enough to invent new ones. Like Salvation."

He looked around. McHugh looked at Espy. Phil read the disbelief written large on McHugh's red face.

"Bullshit."

Harland shrank back, but just as quickly leaned forward toward McHugh.

"Join the crowd. She fools everyone."

McHugh, now on the forward edge of his chair, held his tongue but signaled with a circular motion that Harland should go on. He did, his voice gaining in confidence.

"When she was at BosChem, she was already experimenting with new stuff. She's been using drugs for years. Needs the stuff for her pain, which, by the way, is real. She doesn't have to fake being a cripple. Anyway, she began inventing new drugs for the pain. She's careful, though, not to... you know, overuse. At the same time, she doesn't give a rat's ass for what her inventions do to other people. She thinks the rest of the world is a bunch of losers."

McHugh was still angry. He attacked.

"But she kept you around. That make you a loser, too?"

Harland shrugged.

"What else? Took me in for the sex, mostly. At first."

Harland flashed a proud leer.

"Now *that* I'm good at."

Getting no response, he returned to his account in a resigned voice.

"Sex was a surprise. It comes and goes with her. She kept me around because I could run errands and besides, I was good cover. But that didn't make me less of a loser to her. Maybe more, actually. She could order me around, beat me with that crutch of hers when she felt like it. Lots of times she told me how much she hated me."

McHugh sounded off again, with a disbelieving snort.

"Tell me another one. She's crippled, she's a weak woman, but you stuck around even when she beat you? Big strong drifter like you? You didn't run?"

Harland flared and Phil could see he wasn't faking.

"Easy for you to think you know. I stuck around at first because it was the softest deal I'd ever run into. Later, when Janice's physical condition got worse, she needed more help and that was okay. By the time I learned what she really was, I got afraid. I knew too much. I'm ready to deal because I don't think you guys can bring her in, or, if you do, hold her indefinitely. She'll come after me and she'll never stop until she gets me. Jail's safer than that."

The room was silent for a moment before Espy took over.

"Let's go back to the drugs. You say she was already working on new drugs when you met her. Where did she do her experimenting, at the company?"

Harland calmed down.

"You guys may be after me, but drugs won't get you anywhere on that. Janice ran her drug business on her own. She never told me where exactly, but she had a lab. After I found out what she was really doing, I didn't want to know more about it. She went at night. Always at night. Sometimes all night."

"All of that just to develop drugs to treat her own pain?"

"Yeah, that's what she said when we got together. I don't think it was money. She had enough of that, investments, she told me. I know she began selling some drugs to suppliers in the southwest, in small batches. Like always, she was careful."

"How about the northwest? What brought you up here?"

"Yeah, that was another change, and at first I couldn't figure why. She just announced we were going to make a summer trip up here about three years ago. By the time I knew about it, it was all set up."

"You said 'at first'. Did you find out why?"

Harland fidgeted and looked away. To Phil's ears, his next words sounded hesitant.

"That was a dangerous subject. Janice would get mad when I brought it up."

Espy didn't try to hide his increased interest, leaning forward again.

"What do you mean, dangerous?"

"Dangerous to me. Like there were things about her she didn't want me to know or get into. When I said anything that sounded like I wanted to know more, she'd get mad right away, sometimes throw things. Once she pulled a knife. Like that."

Espy resumed his neutral tone.

"Did you learn anything about why she wanted to come up here?"

"Yeah, maybe one thing. She once said that the plants she used in her drugs weren't right; there was better shit than peyote up in the Cascades. So I thought that our first trip was maybe to get plants."

"Was it?"

"Don't know. I do know that she went out some at night. Wouldn't tell me why, but I was used to that. Only dirt she got me into was boosting a truck in Montana and the plates in Oregon."

Instantly McHugh pounced.

"We're talking about the same truck Lonny was in on the night of Rolf's murder?"

"Yeah, that one."

Espy again.

"How does Lonny Ogden figure into all of this?"

"That's complicated."

"Just tell us what you know. We'll work it out."

"Okay. But how about a break now? I got what they call one of these quick kidneys. Got to pee often."

Espy spoke into the microphone, noting the break for the record. After a uniformed policeman led Casey out of the interrogation room, Phil leaned over to Tom.

"Now we're going to hear about Lonny, do you think it would be a good idea for his sister Calla to listen in, too? Casey might say something that could help us find him, and Lonny seems to be kind of a key to what happened."

Tom turned gruff.

"You can leave it to us to decide what's key."

Phil hoped a grin would set things right.

"I would never presume to think otherwise, Chief. But how about Calla?"

Cisek sighed.

"No objection, except we got a flow going here. Can't risk delaying it for her to get here."

"No problem. I suggested she might hang around here this morning in case she was needed."

Cisek half-bristled.

"You suggested? She's already around here? Didn't we talk about …?"

Cisek paused and subsided.

"… Oh, what the hell, Phil. Eye on the main event. It couldn't hurt. Invite her in."

8:41 AM

Calla awoke to disorientation, not recognizing her surroundings at first. They didn't match the twisted images of her complicated, shifting dreams. Still, she'd gotten more sleep on Phil's couch than she had had for several nights, and could still feel his arms around her, the comforting relaxation that accompanied her directly to slumber.

In the kitchen, a handwritten note from Phil leaned on a flower vase, next to a now-cold cup of coffee.

Morning, dear sleepyhead! I didn't want to wake you and, believe me, it's hard to leave you.

I'll be sitting in on the interview with Harland Casey. Maybe they'll let you sit in, too, and that might help jog your memory about Marie Lowry.

Phil

Marie. The name had intruded off and on, even through deep sleep. She microwaved the cup of coffee and sat in Phil's favorite chair, organizing her case notes and debating whether or not to attend the interview. While she worked, the intrusion arrived again, like a gnat buzzing by her ear.

Suddenly an image blotted out everything else. She sat bolt upright, nearly spilling her coffee. Memories of a dark-haired young woman flooded in, a distant watchful presence, monitoring Calla's young self. She saw herself cringing, and heard her own young, scared voice beg … beg … *Marie* not to hit her again. *Marie's* penetrating, cruel eyes, refused to yield. The scene opened up: Sven Carlson appeared, his shirt unbuttoned, the bead and copper amulet hanging down his chest. Marie cowered before him, then disappeared, and Sven looked disdainfully at young Calla's very pregnant mother.

Seeping slowly back to where she was, Calla caught a last fleeting image of Sven's amulet as his face and his arrogant, drunken smugness faded away.

Frantically she sent Phil a text: *On my way. I remember Marie.*

She left immediately, arriving just as Harland Casey retook his seat. Tom Cisek was grumbling about Casey's unnecessarily long bathroom break. She sat next to Phil, who whispered a quick summary. They both watched the profiles of Espy, McHugh, and Takarchuk behind the glass as they exchanged scribbled notes. The Chief flipped a switch on the wall and, over the speaker, Espy's voice came through clear and strong.

"So, Harland, we were talking about the connection between your wife and Lonny Ogden."

"Yeah, well, it's complicated and I may not have it all right, but I got some ideas."

"Let's hear them."

"Okay, but I can't get to Lonny without saying something about Gabby. The way I see it, the two of them were connected."

"Tell us everything you think is relevant."

"A college kid was the hatchery's night watchman. Job doesn't pay much, so it's mainly been filled with temporaries. One day, the kid says he's leaving the job; the next day, Janice says she's heard that Gabby is available. No way I can prove it, but the way she talked about the change, she seemed happy and I think she fixed it so the kid would leave. I dunno, maybe she paid him, or threatened him. This much I know: Gabby worked for Janice before he came to the hatchery. When he came on as watchman, it was easier to pass product to him. But, because of his duties, he couldn't go out at night; and that's where Lonny came in. I'd hear the truck coming—you know, the Ford 150—and then later he'd leave. Janice once let drop that Lonny knew about native plants, and my guess is she used him to forage for the stuff she needed for Salvation. Over that summer, and this one, Lonny started coming to the hatchery during the day too, and Janice would spend more time with him. Giving him food and telling him stories."

"Why, if Lonny was a nighttime runner, would either one of them risk being seen together in the daytime?"

That was a good question. Calla watched Casey pause and then shift to a different position. He leaned back, looking at the ceiling, before refocusing on his questioners.

"Janice found something special in Lonny. Don't ask me exactly what. But when they were together, I thought they might share a secret of some kind. Janice, see, had no use for Indians. She was always saying bad things about them. About how they were worthless and shifty. Of course, Lonny was part Indian, and when he wasn't around she'd make fun of him, how slow and stupid he was. But when they were together, she'd smile and encourage him. It didn't make sense."

"You've said before that she baked cookies for him."

"Yeah, that was part of the puzzle. Janice wasn't the type to hang around the kitchen. I do—did—the cooking. She started on cookies as a way of delivering her drugs. You know, like LSD or pot in cookies, only this time Salvation. Then she started baking straight cookies, but only for Lonny, 'cause he liked them."

"Are those the same cookies that were poisoned and killed Rolf?"

"A special batch of them, probably, yeah."

Espy pointed Casey to a discrepancy that Calla had noticed, too.

"But you've been telling us about a successful drug operation. Why all of a sudden the need to kill people?"

She watched another change come over Casey. He sagged across the shoulders, expression on his face twisted with the defiance of a cornered animal. It was as if he had finally had enough of the all the different versions of himself. Gone were all traces of the glad-handing salesman, the babbling simpleton overwhelmed by a need to please. A rural twang stole into his voice.

"Like I said once before, all of you got it wrong. Janice puts on a good act, but she's ruthless. She gets rid of anything in her way. And she always gets even."

"Even? Who was she trying to get even with?"

"Never did find out exactly. But it's for something that happened a long time ago. What made her a cripple. I figure it happened up around here. And another thing that took me a while to figure out: she's part Indian. And still she hates Indians—but not all of them, I guess. She could have hurt Lonny any time she wanted; she used to talk about how good it would feel to hurt him. But she didn't. Instead, she seemed to ... to like him, actually. I think she changed her mind about him."

"What do you mean changed?"

Casey took a deep breath and blurted out his answer.

"This is all a guess. She began having these story sessions with Lonny—I overheard parts of them—talking about Indian legends and coyotes and other shit. He loved them, and I think she did too. Janice could pretend she cared, put on a good show. But the longer she hung around Lonny, the more she really cared about him. Like baking cookies."

Silence followed. Calla could tell from Espy's body language that he wasn't sure how to move forward with Casey's revelations. Espy posed his next question softly.

"Take us back to the night Rolf was murdered. What does what you just told us have to do with that?"

Casey threw up his hands, then calmed enough to reply.

"I don't know details. Janice never let me very far into her plans. But I can tell you this: I think she was gradually going crazy. Not running around, seeing green monsters or that kind of thing. What I saw were quick changes in her mood that weren't there before. One day the world was rosy, or at least as rosy as it ever got for Janice. The next day, as if she was in some dark and ugly place. She'd scream at me, hit me with her crutch, swear as dirty as I've ever heard. And it wasn't like anything had happened for her to do that. It was more like she was falling apart."

"My question again, Harland. What about the night of Rolf's murder?"

Casey waved back impatiently.

"Okay. This much I know for sure, because Janice did mention it. She thought someone wanted a bigger piece of the Salvation action. She didn't have proof, but she'd narrowed it down to Rolf and Gabby, maybe the two of them together. The rest I'm just guessing. She probably didn't want Lonny to be around since he was friends with both of them, so she finds him at the Wayside, and gives him a knockout cookie—one that would put him to sleep and get him out of the way. Then she meets Rolf and kills him, planning to take care of Gabby later. She never figured Lonny would be fingered for Rolf's murder."

"That sounds like a lot of detail from someone who was kept in the dark."

Casey glared at Espy.

"I may *play* dumb, but I *ain't* dumb. Fourteen years with a woman and you get to read her pretty well, even if she is an evil bitch. And that's all I got to say to any of you people."

Espy added a touch of sternness.

"I hope you know that we're in charge here and will decide when enough is enough. One more question. Why would Janet, an obviously smart person, put both poison and Salvation into the cookie? The Salvation could lead straight to her. In fact, it already has."

Casey calmed down a little.

"Don't ask me. That's the kind of thing she never—and I *mean never*—let me in on. Maybe there's a time she wouldn't have done that, put Salvation and poison together. But like I told you, if you were listening, she'd become different, out of control. You figure it out."

Espy sat back and dropped the arm, swinging his pen. A half-minute went by. Then the pen came back up and he traded looks with Greg and McHugh. They both nodded.

"Okay, Harland. I want to thank you for your cooperation. We're not done with you yet, but what you've given us is enough for now."

Casey may have stopped, but Calla's emotions were shifting into high gear. She felt disoriented, head swimming. She was trapped in the mixed-up motives of Good Janice/Bad Janice. Of Janice/Marie and of Marie's place in the life of young Calla. It was too much. Pieces of her life, of Lonny's, of others who had affected both of them, projected brightly before her, then flashed away. A kaleidoscope moved in circles around her where there ought to have been a still picture.

Suddenly her subconscious demanded to be heard again, and this time it was shouting the names she needed to bring clarity: Marie! Sven! Pitpit! A single realization jumped out at her. Why hadn't she seen it earlier, it was so obvious? When Sven first came into her home and took up with her mother, he'd brought a daughter with him. Marie had not only been Calla's babysitter; she was Lonny's half-sister.

With immense effort she steadied herself enough to whisper to Chief Cisek.

"Before he leaves, ask him if, in her storytelling, Janice mentioned 'Stick-showers'."

Cisek looked at her, startled then skeptical. He replied out loud. "Sure this is important?"

She was glad he simply asked the question and hadn't asked for an explanation. She didn't have a coherent one herself. She raised her voice to match the Chief's.

"Yes, I'm sure."

The Chief spoke into the microphone connected to Espy's earpiece. Espy rose and shooed everyone back to their places. When Casey sat and the motion around him settled, Espy asked him about Stick-showers.

Casey didn't have to think long, and responded with a quizzical look on his face.

"Yeah she did, but I had no idea what that was about. Only thing I could tell was that most of the time Lonny had this happy look. Especially when Janice was telling animal stories. But when she brought up the Stick-showers, he looked scared and kind of curled up in a ball. Weird, I thought. Why do you ask?"

Calla heard every word of Casey's answer. But her concentration was now on McHugh. He had turned around and was looking at the one-way mirror.

As if he were staring directly at her.

11:40 AM

Greg felt an electric current, a tangible excitement, in the air after the uniformed deputy led Casey back to his cell. The case had broken wide open and they had their prime suspect; now they needed to find her.

McHugh shot a glance toward Greg. No anger now, just urgency, but with the same intensity. His words didn't let that show, though, when he turned to Espy.

"Climbin' the wrong tree. Recalibration time."

Espy nodded.

"Looks like Janice told Lonny to tie her up in Bianchi's house. They're playing on the same team, but I don't think any jury in the world is going to think Lonny masterminded any of it. We won't know anything for sure until we find them. Any ideas?"

McHugh sucked on his teeth.

"I'm guessing here. All that storytelling with Lonny wasn't just to entertain him. The stories have messages. That much I know, though I never paid much attention to them when I was a kid. Some of them designate particular places. Suppose Janice used to the stories to direct Lonny where to pick up and drop off drugs, what plants to find, and maybe where they were supposed to meet if they had to run for it. They both could be there now."

Espy didn't hide the fact that he was dubious.

"Pretty thin. And without a lead on a location, we've got nothing. You got any strong feelings about actual places?"

"No, not yet. But I think I know how to get one."

"How?"

"I had an aunt at the Pitpit rez and visited the place a few times. There was this young guy who took the old stories seriously, spent a lot of time with the older folks, writing down their versions. He shouldn't be more than about sixty now. I can find out pretty quick whether he's still alive. Don't know his real name; we all called him 'Story Man'. If he's still around, I could drive up there and back today, and see if there are any special places associated with the Stick-showers. Or if he knew Janice when she was still Marie. I can't call, because this guy liked to live off the grid. He allowed himself electricity, but no phone. Doubt if that's changed. I know it's thin, but if he gives us something, we could check it out."

Espy looked down at his notes. Greg got the impression he wasn't studying them so much as deciding. When he was ready, Espy set things in motion.

"Okay, Bill, see if you can find your Story Man. I'll see if Cisek will let Greg go with you. Meanwhile, I'll activate the usual channels to find out if there's any trace of Janice Casey. Better get moving."

Greg watched McHugh step off to the side by Calla Ogden. They talked while Espy sought out the Chief. Calla handed something to McHugh. Minutes later, Cisek gave his permission.

Greg hurried after McHugh and they took off in McHugh's unmarked car. Soon they left the main highway and followed a narrow rising road hemmed in by dark green forest. Forty-five minutes after they started, McHugh broke their silence.

"You waiting for me to admit I was wrong about Ferris?"

"No."

He had his eyes on McHugh, who kept his own eyes on the curves and upward thrusts of the road.

"You might be right that Ferris wasn't the killer this time. Doesn't mean he wasn't before, or that he won't be again. He's still dirty in my book. We went by his place. Locked up tight and no car. He must have taken off. Any idea where?"

"Why should I have an idea?"

"You and him seemed to be getting pretty tight."

He'd had enough. Some of his own anger probably showed, though he tried to stay calm.

"Ferris gets into anything dirty in the future, I'm on him just like anyone else. Meantime, we've got a real suspect to find, in case you forgot."

McHugh kept his eyes on the road, though his tone leveled some.

"You still got a lot to learn. And it looks like you want to learn the hard way. That's up to you. But, okay. We got a job to do."

Steamed, he willed himself to speak as if he'd heard a concession.

"How do you want to handle it?"

McHugh switched, sounding now like a cop just tending to business.

"Calla Ogden had another piece of information, an object that might help us unlock Story Man's memory."

Without slowing down, McHugh fished in his pocket and handed over a leather thong with an amulet attached. McHugh told Greg what Calla knew about it.

"So I try to find the Story Man, show him this amulet and see what he can tell us. While I do that, you can check around to see if anyone remembers Sven Carlson and his daughter. That's as far as you can go. No one will tell you anything more."

"Because I'm white?"

"Because you're a stranger and you're not native. Amounts to the same thing."

"And you'll go back to being native enough to get information."

McHugh's eyes left the road and blazed with anger.

"Watch it!"

Greg knew he'd let his own anger push him too far.

"That came out wrong. Sorry."

They traveled another thirty miles in silence, eventually stopping at a gas station. McHugh wore his cop face again.

"Wait here while I find out where to go."

McHugh walked past two gas pumps and entered a convenience store. Greg stepped out of the car and stretched. Beyond its parking area stood a fading sign which, in large letters surrounded by exploding fireworks, announced that the "new, exciting Pitpit Casino" would open soon. McHugh said the sign had been there for over three years and that the casino application was all but dead. Except for that sign and another one a mile back that had announced their entry to the Pitpit reservation, nothing set this stretch of road apart from the seventy-plus miles they'd traveled.

McHugh was back within five minutes carrying two paper cups of coffee, and holding one out to him. He took it as a peace offering. They drove about a mile into the woods on an asphalt ribbon that was in bad repair and barely wide enough for two cars to pass each other. Not that there was much traffic. They saw a dozen houses at most, small places, some neat and well-tended, several with large, junk-littered yards. McHugh slowed near three of the houses. At each one he offered a variation of the same comment.

"Someone here might remember Sven Carlson."

A dirt road went even deeper into the woods. They parked at a stream. One wooden plank extended to a boulder in midstream and a second plank linked the boulder to the other side. Greg followed McHugh across and along a trail until they could see a cabin with a figure standing warily in front of it. He was thin, with two long gray braids and a weather-beaten face. A straw cowboy hat topped mismatched clothes.

McHugh halted them.

"Go back to the houses I showed you and see what you can find out about Sven. When you're done, come pick me up here. No cell signal out here. As fallback, we'll meet at the convenience store."

Greg backtracked, parked, and had to weave through two old refrigerators and assorted car parts to the rickety porch of the first house. No one was home.

The second house was one of the tidy ones. He knocked and an elderly lady with braided hair, clad in a clean bathrobe, answered the door. After introducing himself, he ventured a polite question.

"Do you remember a Sven Carlson living around here twenty or twenty-five years back?"

The woman carefully maintained a blank expression. She stared at him for a long time, slowly nodded and slowly closed the door. As it closed, Greg managed a departing comment through the crack.

"Thanks for your attention. I may be back later with a fellow officer."

The last house was empty too, so Greg drove back to the stream, parked and waited.

A half hour later, McHugh came out of the trees and walked across the planks toward him.

"What did you get?"

"Just one lady who remembers Carlson. But she wasn't talking to me."

"That's okay. Maybe she will with me. Let's go."

"Wait a sec. What did you get from Story Man?"

McHugh settled back against the car seat.

"Okay. The Story Man remembers Sven Carlson, Marie Lowry, Calla and Lonny Ogden. He recognized the amulet, and even remembered me as a kid. Mainly he knows people in relation to the old stories. Marie and Calla, along with other kids, would come by—me, too, once in a while—and he'd spin out the legends. Sven would sometimes be there with Marie. Never said anything, according to Story Man, and paid no special attention most of the time."

"Sounds like all that's not much help."

"You're right. But it might fit in if I can learn more from the lady here."

He looked out the window for a long moment, back toward the creek and the cabin.

"Funny about coming back here. Makes me remember all kinds of things."

Greg heard something different from McHugh's usual gruffness: a hint of nostalgia—and even pain?

They drove back to the old lady's house and saw her curtains move.

Greg waited while McHugh disappeared into the house. After several minutes, he got out and alternately perched on the front bumper or leaned against the fender. Almost an hour after he had entered the house, McHugh reappeared moving quickly toward the car. He called to Greg when he was only halfway across the front yard.

"Your phone have a signal?"

Greg checked.

"Nope."

"Then we need to get to the convenience store. They've got a land line. My talk with the old lady was worth more than I thought it would be. Now we gotta move fast."

At the convenience store, McHugh rushed inside. Greg imagined several possible reasons for the visible agitation, but tried to keep from focusing on any of them until he had the facts.

McHugh ran out the door, pulled the Garmin GPS from their vehicle and tapped in coordinates. He worked too fast, made a mistake, held the unit by his side while he breathed deeply, and started over. The store owner, a plump, fiftyish woman in jeans and a silvery top styled to resemble a buckskin shirt, appeared with a paper bag. She handed it through the window to Greg as McHugh finished with the GPS.

"Food. Come back sometime."

Greg glanced into the bag at sandwiches, fruit, and chips and thanked the woman sincerely. He slipped into the driver's seat and pulled the car to the gas pumps. By the time Greg finished filling the tank, McHugh had the GPS back in its holder and had pulled bills from his wallet to give to the store lady.

When they were on a road heading northeast, McHugh began to talk.

"Our best bet is that Janice Casey and Lonny are at Setakit Creek. The Kittinach Sheriff is working with his counterpart in Chenogan County, and he's coming up by helicopter."

"So we're in an emergency situation?"

"Maybe, maybe not."

Greg waited for McHugh to go on and, when he didn't, prompted him.

"You got specific information out of your last interview?"

"Information, yeah. Not exactly specific, but enough to act on."

McHugh took his eyes off the road to throw a searching glance in his direction.

"Story Man told me that the only time Sven, Marie's father paid attention was when Story Man talked about the Stick-showers. All the native stories have got action, and some have danger. But the real scary ones are always about the Stick-showers. They're like White ghost stories. If you know what I mean."

He did, and nodded. He suspected that McHugh might be wondering whether he had to explain American references to a Ukrainian immigrant. McHugh was already going on.

"That's about all Story Man could tell me, apart from the fact that he'd heard that Sven liked to tell Stick-shower stories to the kids, usually making them more scary. Story Man didn't like Sven, and even asked him to stop coming around, but Sven went on showing up if he felt like it."

"Where's the cause for emergency in all that?"

"None. The real valuable stuff came from the older lady, Amanda Shays. She's not in good health and doesn't get around now. But she still talks, and I mean a lot. I bet in her day she was the center for all the gossip. She also knew Sven and Marie and Calla. Had no use for Sven. He had no Indian blood, but at first lived nearby. When he was orphaned, he began to hang out on the rez. Kinda lived with one family, then another. Could be charming, but also mean. He got a girl on the reservation pregnant when she was fifteen, and Marie was the result. Marie's mother was sickly and eventually died young. Sven spent a lot of time out with the men, drinking and finding other women. Marie went to get him one evening when he and his friends were drinking. She was maybe nine. What started out like a prank to scare her turned ugly, and Marie got badly injured. The Indian guys were involved. Sven didn't take her to the doctor. She became crippled, and had to use a crutch. Sven started calling her Stick Girl."

"She must have hated him."

"Oh yeah, him and the Indians who beat on her. Amanda described her about the way Casey did—a loner, smart, calculating. Amanda said that when she heard about Sven's death, she had no doubt at all that Marie—Janice now—was behind it, proof or no proof. Besides—my point, not Amanda's—how else could she have gotten Sven's amulet?"

"I'm still not seeing how what you learned connects to where we are now."

"The key is Lonny. Put your head around this. When Marie's about 18, Sven takes up with Calla's mother. Sven turns her into an alcoholic and gives her a baby boy, Lonny, who comes out damaged, although no one realizes it at first. Sven stays close for a few months, shows off his son, brags about how strong and perfect he is. And especially likes to brag publically in front of 'Stick Girl'."

"I think I see where this is going."

McHugh nodded as he urged the car to greater speed.

"Yeah, it's based on flimsy evidence, but still our best bet. Sven hangs around long enough to see how retarded Lonny really is, and then takes off. Marie goes her own way and becomes a chemist, becomes Janice, still with a grudge against Indians, and against Sven and Lonny, the people she hates the most."

"That's what I had in mind; but where are we going, right now, so fast? And why?"

"In the stories, the Stick-showers used two places—they're called the staircases—as tests of strength and endurance. Those were places to flirt with danger, to prove your manhood. One is down on the Columbia River and the other is where we're going. It may or may not be the right guess, but it's the one that makes most sense."

"A story? We're going somewhere because of a story?"

He could hear his own incredulity, but McHugh was undeterred.

"Not because of the story but because of the story's location. If I'm right, we should find Janice Casey and Lonny, both at the same place."

"Pretty neat, if true. Wraps up a lot. But what in the story makes you think we'll find them?"

"It goes like this. Janice—Marie back then—hears a lot about the Stick-showers because her father likes to scare kids with them. Recently, she'd told some of the same stories to Lonny. Lonny may not have liked those Stick-shower stories, but he did pay attention to them. So if Janice wanted to give Lonny a location to meet in case everything went wrong, he would know where the staircases are. The staircase up ahead of us is the best bet."

"And how does she get there?"

"She's got the pickup, remember?"

"Okay, maybe. But *why?* She ought to be heading away from the state if she wants to escape."

"If Harland Casey's right, Janice is going crazy and she's got mixed feelings about Lonny. She wants to punish him, or wants to use him to get revenge on a father she still hates. But she also likes Lonny. Loves him, maybe, if she can love anyone. Maybe the only escape she sees is to end it for both of them, especially at a symbolic place. It's not worth taking a chance that that's what she intends to do."

"Could be completely wrong, too."

Defensiveness and some anger tinged McHugh's gruff response.

"If you've got a better idea just say so. Otherwise, let's shut up and get there."

The landscape whizzed past them. They'd started their trip amid Doug firs, which gave way mainly to Ponderosas. Almost an hour ago, those, too, were gone, replaced by stubbier evergreens and occasional stretches of flats and scrub brush. When they paralleled water, they traveled beside broad swaths of green along tributaries that wound their way toward a final merging with the big Columbia.

Ahead they might find only more trees and rocks and water, or else the ominous encounter with danger that the old stories predicted.

7:01 PM

Calla, leaning over to stretch her tight hamstrings, got an upside-down look at the slowing rotor of the six-man helicopter that she had just exited. She straightened to see the Kittinach Sheriff, Collins, a trim figure of average height, talking with Sheriff Barlow from Chenogan County, a rawboned string bean with a full head of sandy hair. Behind him, another man was sorting through an open box of climbing equipment. Off to the side stood Phil.

Greg Takarchuk and Bill McHugh had been there already, when the helicopter landed in a fallow farm field about a hundred yards away from where Setakit Creek joined with one of the larger tributaries of the Columbia River. Before landing, Calla had seen from above how the tributary flowed east, full and powerful, and, on the surface, deceptively placid. The smaller Setakit Creek, she knew, started as a series of mountain streams that dropped into a U-shaped valley to unite in a rushing torrent. Now swollen with a late spring run-off, the Setakit had to pass one last constricted channel before giving up its roiling load to the tributary and, eventually, to the Columbia.

Flat land ran toward the Serakit's bank, then rose two hundred feet or so above the river to the top of a round geologic upthrust. Dwarfed though it was by mountains to the west, the rise was still the highest point in their immediate vicinity. She had never been here before, although she knew that in the old days her forebears had traveled the Setakit into the mountains in search of game. Now the sight of that rise above the creek merged with her imagination of a legendary place in the old stories: the staircase of the Stick-showers.

She walked over to Phil.

"Anything yet?"

"We're waiting. Other officers across the river have a scope on the face of that big hill and they're scanning it now."

"I still don't see what we can do, even if Janice and Lonny are there. There's no sign of Casey's pickup, though I guess it could be parked in any of the stands of trees around here."

She felt her spirits sink. When sudden arrangements had led to her actually being in the helicopter, possibly heading toward Lonny, she had experienced a surge of optimism. Now that she saw the harsh landscape and the water barrier, she wondered how she could have been so naïve as to hope for any kind of easy, happy conclusion.

Phil gently squeezed her shoulder.

"It's too early to get discouraged. Sheriff Barlow warned us that it would take time to find out whether Janice and Lonny are here, much less do anything about it. Tell me again the symbolic importance of the rise over there."

She knew he was just making talk, trying to divert her. But why not?

"It's a place where important decisions were made. There's a bigger one like it down on the Oregon side of the Columbia, the Big Staircase. This one is called the Little Staircase. They both worked the same way. On your way home from a trip, you could take your chances with the Stick-showers. If you climbed the staircase successfully, you were guaranteed to get home safely. If you tried and failed, something bad would happen to you. You could increase your good luck by climbing with water in your mouth, and not drinking it until you got back down. If you swallowed it…well, you can guess."

"Do you believe that Janice would come here?"

"I don't know what to believe. One side of me says that if she's still that troubled young woman from the reservation, she might. The staircase could have a pull on her. Another voice tells me she left the native life a long time back and wouldn't have any use for those old stories, except maybe to entertain Lonny."

Sheriff Barlow called them over.

"So far, still no sightings from the spotters on the other side. We're going to climb along the river side of that rock hill there and get a direct view. You can stay here if you want, or come along. Just keep well back and out of the way if anything develops."

She looked up at the rock hill. The slope was gradual at first but grew steeper near the top. From where they stood, the surface was like a smooth ball—dark basalt, Phil told her—not as craggy and broken as the mountains behind Swiftwater and Portal. It was an easy walk to the base of the hill.

When they came around the hill the view changed dramatically. From a distance, the old story about the Stick-showers' staircase had sounded tame. Looking now along the exposed path that her ancestors had scaled for centuries, the story possessed a stark and immediate presence. A third of the big ball was gone, leaving an almost vertical face slanting steeply toward the water. At the base of the half-ball an outcropping hung over the river, where water boiled through rocky rapids. Jagged boulders, parts of the hill that had broken off a long time ago, clustered randomly where the outcropping joined the base of the hill.

She moved closer to McHugh, who was gesticulating toward the massive rise, explaining its features and access. He had to speak loudly to be heard over the sound of rushing water.

"Those indentations up there are like a zigzag path when you get on them. That's the staircase the natives used to climb. There's only two ways up. From down below and from here. Down below, you got access to the whole staircase, up and down. From here, you have to climb horizontally and up some across the face to get on the staircase at about the halfway point. Then you can go up to the top or down to the river."

Sheriff Barlow pointed.

"How about from the other side of the hill?"

"If you really know your way around rocks, you can work your way down from there to the outcrop by the river. But it's real tricky."

"Anything else I should know?"

"Yeah. That outcrop's very slippery. The surface is only about five feet above the water. Looks nice and level from here, but it's got quite a slant, and it's always wet. We've had to make rescues here; a few years back, two people died."

"It's looking less and less like a crippled woman and an inexperienced climber would choose to come to this place."

She began to relax. What would mean a wild goose chase for others would bring temporary relief to her. She might not know where Janice and Lonny had gone, but at least they hadn't come to this forbidding place. Her watch showed just after 7 p.m. Another hour and the sun would disappear behind the Cascades. A half-hour after that, darkness would seep in.

Her gaze strayed toward the area where McHugh had said the trail started. The dark green of a bush contrasted with nearly black basalt. There was more blackness peeking out from under the bush, different from the rock. She took a few tentative steps toward the object and then recognized it. Fear rose like a gorge in her throat.

She was looking at tubular metal. At a crutch. The last time she had seen it, that object had been attached to Janice Casey's arm.

7:14 PM

Greg watched Barlow, the Sheriff from Chenogan County, answer a walkie-talkie. After a few seconds, his head snapped down toward the outcropping below them. He peered at the scene before responding.

"Don't see anyone from here."

A pause, then a decisive conclusion.

"We'll start over that way."

Still holding the walkie-talkie in one hand, Barlow motioned for the law enforcement personnel around him to draw closer. His eyes were on Sheriff Collins, but the words were for everyone.

"Okay, the spotters across the river have seen definite movement at the back of the outcropping. They have identified a human leg in jeans and the back of a head they believe to be female. Both persons are alive, though it's impossible to be certain of their condition or whether they are armed."

He shifted his gaze to each person in turn.

"How many of you have climbed this route before?"

McHugh and one other officer, a dark-haired compact man.

"Okay, McHugh, you're the most experienced climber here. You lead the way."

McHugh moved a step closer to Barlow.

"I could do that, but I've got a suggestion."

"Make it quick."

"Lopez, here, knows this place and would get you down to the river's edge just fine. At the bottom, before you come out on the overhang, you're in a narrow spot without maneuverability. Like corks in a bottle. I can get around to the other side of this hill and make the shorter approach from there. It gives us another option if anything unexpected happens."

Barlow thought that over, his prominent Adam's apple making several round trips.

"How long would that take?"

"I'd get there about the same time as the rest of you."

This time Barlow did not hesitate.

"Okay. You do that. Now, we all better get going."

The men helped themselves to rope and other equipment in the box. McHugh slung an extra-long length of coiled climbing rope over one shoulder and below his arm on the opposite side. Greg, putting on climbing gloves, caught one last glimpse of McHugh moving fast around the back of the hill.

Then he was hurrying to catch up with Barlow and the others, testing the rock's tricky surface, trying to feel it through his feet and his fingers.

7:31 PM

Everyone was gone except Sheriff Collins, Calla and himself. Phil spoke briefly with Collins, who announced he was going back to the helicopter. From there, the Sheriff would be able to stay in closer touch with possible back-up resources.

Phil watched the lawman trudge off. He also watched Calla try to sit still. She perched on the equipment box, but a moment later began pacing again. He waited and, as he expected, soon heard her arrive at the point where she couldn't take it any longer.

"I should be down there. What am I going to do up here? Just wait? Suppose they do need me. I'd never get there in time."

All of the frustration and pressure of the last week concentrated in her outburst. He didn't react in kind; she burned with a flame that needed no extra fuel.

"Might be. But maybe not. We could just get in the way."

"I was talking about me."

"And I wouldn't let you try that trail by yourself."

She stopped to look squarely at him.

"You'd be willing to come along?"

"Sure I would. Wouldn't have it any other way. On one condition."

"What?"

"If it gets too dangerous, we come back. And you let me decide if that time comes."

She hesitated. Did she want to make her own decision? Did she think he intended to go a short distance and cancel?

In a few seconds she decided.

"I agree."

"Okay, then. If we're going to do it, let's do it."

Over the next ten minutes they traversed the rock face on a path exactly as McHugh had described it. Phil couldn't see more than a few feet ahead on the slanting face that was already in shadow. The way was clear, but you had to trust it in small increments. Footing was solid enough, though hand holds were difficult to find and he watched Calla, ahead of him, leaning into the slope for support. He did the same.

They ascended gradually until their path took a sharp upward turn and then stopped. They had reached the vertical path, the staircase, more clearly visible than the sideways one they had been on. One part of the bigger trail zigged upward, while a second one zagged down. On the downward leg, they caught sight of Barlow and his party about halfway to the outcropping. Progress from that point on was easier, partly because they were going downhill and partly because they had a better view of where they were going. They still had to focus on the area immediately in front of them; a misstep could cost them serious injury. Phil hoped Calla was being as careful as he was. But he could see her looking anxiously beyond their shifting position, at their destination.

With each step down the steep trail, he felt a sinking feeling of another kind. He saw not only Calla in the trail, but, in his mind's eye, the face of his former wife in her last hours. Life vying with death. The loss of one loved one reminding him that he could not, would not lose another. But what kind of choice might he have to make down below? Could Calla and Lonny both be saved? He didn't want to face that choice, yet knew he had already made it; and that the price of choosing might be almost as high as the price of losing someone.

He forced his concentration back to the trail, dimming, but not completely banishing, those darker thoughts.

The farther they descended, the louder grew the sound of rushing water. He thought he could feel spray on his face, though he knew that cool feeling might also mean that he was sweating and the wind was picking up, as it often did when darkness approached.

They were almost to the bottom when the trail broadened and made a sharp turn. They emerged onto a ledge above a larger outcropping about ten feet below. On the right, their ledge became a small cliff, dropping about twenty feet straight down to the creek and its rapids. On the left, a narrow trail, with several quick switchbacks though large boulders, led down to the outcropping. Jumping onto the outcropping from the ledge was a possibility, though he could see now how wet the outcropping was. The narrow trail through the boulders meant that individuals could get to the lower surface only in single file. There would be no opportunity for a concerted rush.

Barlow, Greg, and Lopez were already on the ledge. Though Barlow said nothing, it was easy to see from the look on his face that he was not pleased to see Phil and Calla. He flashed them a warning glance, then snapped his attention back to where the others were nervously watching the scene not far in front of them.

On the edge of the outcropping, her legs dangling over, sat Janice Casey. Her arm was around Lonny seated close beside her. Lonny, his face visible over Janice's shoulder, looked toward the rear of the overhang, then upward. Lonny must have seen Calla because he began to struggle, and then to shout.

Over the roar of the churning water, disconnected fragments of Lonny's words reached them.

"… don't want to … water cold … Calla … Calla …"

Phil turned to gauge Calla's reaction, but he was too late. She was already moving, running across the ledge toward the descending switchback trail, shouting Lonny's name.

From below, Janice swiveled her torso and looked up to see not just Calla running toward her, but the others on the ledge as well. Her mouth twisted into a cruel grimace and she sneered in Calla's direction while pulling Lonny even closer, leaning toward the rushing water below.

7:48 PM

The moment one foot landed on the overhang and began to slide away, Calla knew she should have been more cautious. The image of Lonny being held by that horrible woman had overcome her rational thinking. She tried to slow herself, shifting weight to her rear foot, still on the trail, but the maneuver only threw her more off balance. She slammed into one of the boulders and, as she began to slide by it, instinctively reached for a grip. She found one, just enough to stop her momentum and to keep her from pitching onto a steeper part of the shelf.

Panting and disoriented, she righted herself, looked around, and found Janice about ten yards away. While the whole shelf hung over the river, a small section of it jutted out an extra four feet. Janice was on that extreme perch, her legs only a few feet above the swirling water and the rocks. Lonny struggled in Janice's grasp, his eyes filled with terror.

Her brother's fearful face was like an electric shock, and Calla fought the spontaneous abandon and irrationality that arrived with it. She levered her body into a cross-legged position up against the boulders at the back side of the overhang. Janice threw mocking words across the gap between them.

"So, beautiful little Calla joins us. Too bad there's no one here to tell you how cute and smart you are."

Calla tried to recall the dark-haired babysitter who had once cared for her, but the haggard figure sitting there emitted such a powerful anger that any pleasant memories would have died instantly.

"Janice … Marie … stop. Let Lonny go."

The sound of the river drowned out subtleties. A snarl distorted Janice's face even more.

"You prissy bitch. I'm not letting him go."

Lonny jerked and Janice gripped his neck tighter each time Lonny tried to push her away. Their perch was now only a few inches short of the edge over the river.

Calla felt panic rising inside, and pushed hard against it.

"Why not let him go? It's me you hate. But why?"

Janice's voice rose and Calla could now hear every word distinctly.

"So now you're interested, but it's too late."

"Too late for what?"

"For anyone to care."

Sadness brushed briefly across Janice's face before defiance returned in full force.

"Your whore of a mother lured my father away. He was a drunk and a bastard and he beat me and laughed at me. The rest of you, you did nothing, didn't care. Typical Indians. Live and let live. Care for yourselves, but for no one else."

Calla was stunned by the venom. She'd met people this deluded in her line of work, and knew that reasoning with them was almost impossible. Was there any sympathy left in Janice?

"What did you expect of me? I was only a girl. What could I have done?"

No answer.

"Indians, natives, Native Americans. Call us what you want. We're people, good and bad, just like everyone else. You and me and Lonny are all part Indian."

Janice cackled.

"You, yes. Lonny, too, sorry to say. But not me. Not anymore. I was given the blood, but I gave myself a transfusion. Purged myself. Got beyond Indian."

"And then you got even."

Smugness joined in.

"You might say that. It was just a matter of using my brain, making something they'd fall for, and enjoy. The Indians and the white trash did the rest, using it, wanting more, finding one more way to ruin themselves. Thinking they'd found salvation."

A bitter laugh cut through a gust of wind, and Calla tried once more to reach whatever might be left of Janice's better instincts.

"He's your brother, Janice, whether you like it or not. And you cared for him enough to give him your father's amulet."

That was all the persuasiveness Calla could muster. She choked up.

"And he's my brother and I don't want him to die."

Janice's face became a battlefield of doubt and indecision.

"That's the problem, isn't it? My brother could live. I might be able to purge him, save him. But *your* brother's no better than you are. Better off dead."

Janice made a show of pulling Lonny close. After his earlier struggle, Lonny seemed to have sunk into passive acceptance. Janice leaned back to look at him, as if he were some kind of specimen, pushed him away and immediately clutched him back. Defiance returned, stronger than before, now armored in heavy sarcasm.

"Have you got any more special social service techniques to calm me? Or are you going to try to coax information out of me for the benefit of the police up there?"

Janice looked up. Calla didn't, but imagined the officers standing close to the lip of the shelf, their weapons probably drawn. She didn't have time to think of a response before Janice went on in a voice that rose almost to a scream.

"Well it's over. Nothing you can say will change anything. Lonny's got no life here. Maybe there's one where we're going."

Janice's hold on Lonny changed from embrace to unyielding grip. She leaned outward over the water. Lonny struggled again, but his flailing only made their position more precarious. They both began to slide.

Calla rose in panic, ready to throw herself forward, when a movement at the corner of her eyesight distracted her. Some large object was falling toward Janice and Lonny. She could not figure out what it was.

She only knew that it would be too little and too late.

8:11 PM

Lopez had spotted him first, and nudged Greg, pointing. Then Greg saw him too: McHugh, holding a rope and making his way across the rock face to the boulders just above where Janice held Lonny. Along with Barlow and Lopez, Greg had been watching the scene from about ten feet above, hearing fragments of the conversation between Calla and Janice, trying to piece together the rest. Barlow wisely held them back. Any sudden movement and Janice would fall into the river, deliberately or not, in either case pulling Lonny with her.

McHugh reached the top of one of the boulders and appeared to pause to select his next move. In the fading light it was difficult to see, but it looked as if McHugh had no more rope. He was holding onto the end as he leaned outward to get a better view. A sudden gust of wind must have increased the precariousness of his position. One of his feet began to slip and the next moment he was falling down the front of the boulder, landing with a thud that carried over the river's noise, along with the sound of something breaking.

Greg didn't wait to see more and immediately launched himself downward. It was a tricky jump to a slippery surface under any conditions. Deepening shadow robbed him of his depth perception; he hit the surface too hard and too soon. His feet slipped away and he fell into an awkward sprawl, his head toward the river.

Even slightly dazed, he knew he was sliding. Instinct and mental preparation were all he had—that and the rubberized gloves he'd pulled from the equipment box. He spread both hands and pushed them against the surface, willing the tiny balls and indentations on the gloves' palms to slow him. At the same time, he pushed the toes of his boots down, asking the same of them.

All his concentration was used up in slowing forward momentum, so when he stopped he wasn't sure where he was. He raised his head, trying not to move anything else. McHugh was about six feet to his left. He could see that one of the big man's feet was caught in a crevice between two boulders and the leg that extended from it was twisted at an unnatural angle. An arm hung limply down, blood oozing through the long-sleeve shirt at the elbow. But McHugh's other hand gripped Lonny Ogden's right ankle. Lonny was fighting off Janice who still had an arm around his shoulder, pulling him toward the river.

Greg squirmed toward McHugh, felt himself begin to slip and recalibrated, compromising speed for control. Seconds felt like minutes. He reached a place parallel to and slightly forward of McHugh. They might all pitch into the river, but he saw one slim chance. He yelled to McHugh.

"Bill! Grab my ankle."

McHugh looked at him with glazed eyes; Greg had to hope he heard.

"Okay... One... Two... Three!"

Simultaneously, Greg reached out his left arm and grabbed Lonny's left wrist. At that instant, he felt McHugh's hand on his left ankle. He yanked on Lonny's arm, noticed some give and raised his head enough to see Janice, losing her balance as she lost hold of Lonny. He thought he saw surprise on her face, but whatever it was disappeared as her body slid over the edge and into the raging river.

He shouted to Lonny.

"Don't move!"

Barlow and Lopez would figure out something. All he had to do was make sure that he and Lonny and McHugh hung on until then.

He looked over at McHugh and saw that the man's head had begun to droop; McHugh's grip on his ankle was weakening.

At that moment, he felt a strong pull on his arm and heard Lonny yell.

"Janice!"

McHugh's grip was completely gone. Lonny pulled toward the river and Greg tightened his hold on Lonny's wrist. But Lonny was falling, and Greg slid with him, faster and faster toward the edge until they both went over.

8:12 PM

Calla was up and moving forward, toward Lonny and the roiling river, when Phil bear-hugged her from behind. Surprise made her go stiff, but only for a second. Adrenaline gave her a strength that took Phil by surprise. She struggled like a person twice her size, and he felt himself being pulled along with her. He shifted his feet, found a slight purchase and aimed his weight back toward the boulders. Both of them were falling, but at least not in the direction of the river.

As soon as he had seen Calla run down to the overhang, he had moved laterally away from the officers and scuttled down the narrow switchbacks until he stood a yard or two behind her. When Janice began her slide into the water, and Calla had reacted instinctively to save her brother, he moved to save the woman he loved.

Now he was on top of her, legs spread on the surface to keep from sliding. Calla writhed beneath him, fists hitting the ground, trying to reach him. His mouth was by her ear.

"Calla, Calla. Stop!"

Her yell was muffled by the stone surface, but lost none of its desperation.

"Get off! Let me go! I've got to help him."

"You can't. You'll only hurt yourself."

"I don't care. Get off."

"Trust me."

Each time she moved, there was less energy. Her garbled words gave way to wracking sobs. He raised his head. McHugh lay completely still. And Greg and Lonny were gone.

Another nearby movement caught his eye. He turned his head to see Lopez crawling on hands and knees toward the lip of the overhang. A rope circled his chest below his arms, trailing back to the end of the switchbacks a yard or two behind. There Barlow played out the rope, one leg planted at chest height against a boulder.

Calla stopped sobbing long enough to let out an anguished question.

"Can you see? Is Lonny still all right?"

There were moments when truth would hurt more than help. This was one of them.

"He'll be fine."

His heart felt like ground glass. She would never trust him again.

8:14 PM

Water hit him from all sides, cancelling one direction while it drove him in another. Greg fought for his life—and Lonny's—as they were shoved and pulled and spun all at once. The rest was overwhelming numbness in a freezing liquid world that had no top or bottom. He knew Lonny was with him only because Greg still held tight to Lonny's wrist, clutched it as if it were a lifeline.

They slammed into a hard surface. Instinct combined with desperation; his free hand tried for a hold. He found one for a second, then lost it as the river ripped them away. Their spin slowed, and a flash view gave Greg a glimpse of less violent water closer to the bank. With the next water surge, he took a stroke in that direction. Then another. A rough rock appeared and he grabbed at it. Got a grip. Managed to hold on.

Then his attention shifted to Lonny. The slight young man was flailing with his free arm, his head mostly underwater, bobbing up randomly for air. Greg pulled him closer and yelled.

"Grab my shoulder."

Nothing. Again the same command. He saw Lonny try twice, start to give up, and then, catching help from a shift in the water's movement, throw his right hand around Greg's neck. Greg immediately felt the new, awkward pressure weaken his hold on the rock. Lonny's ear was close and his head now completely above water. He told Lonny what to do and got a nod in reply. It would be a tricky maneuver, but it was their only chance to keep from being swept back into the main surge.

Greg rotated so he faced the rock, moving Lonny's left arm across his own chest. He shouted a three-count and on "three", let go of Lonny's hand and reached with his own now-free left hand for a second purchase on the rock. As he grappled past one place that didn't work and found another, he felt Lonny's left arm join the right one around his neck.

Now he had two hands on the rock. But Lonny, in his desperation, was tightening his grip around Greg's throat with both arms.

"Stop ... ease up!"

His commands got, if anything, more pressure. He tried to maintain his hold on the rock, but his fingers were slipping. Slipping away just like Olga was slipping away from him. She suddenly appeared beside him, observing. How he wanted her to reach out and help him. Her eyes were so sympathetic.

Olga began to fade. His numb fingers signaled that they had no more to give. Vaguely he became aware of something passing under his arm, but hadn't the energy to give it any real attention. The river's rough water beckoned as he moved faster and faster toward it. With inconsolable regret, he thought one last time about Olga.

He and Lonny were swept into the maelstrom. But suddenly they stopped moving downstream, holding one place with the river roaring around them.

His hands went instinctively to his neck and forced his fingers under Lonny's encircling arms. He was able to ease the pressure just enough so he could breathe again. Consciousness returned, but he couldn't understand what had happened. They definitely had stopped moving. A different pressure, one he hadn't realized before, circled his chest. A rope. He tried to wrench around for a look, but couldn't turn against the force of the water.

Then he heard a voice above the roaring.

"Take it easy. It's me, Lopez. The rope's around all three of us. The helicopter's on its way."

Greg drifted. The freezing, uncertain water boiled around them, and he felt both himself and Lonny begin to shiver.

"We'll be okay, Lonny, just hold on."

He tried to take his own advice, but mentally he was slipping away, imagining himself no longer in freezing water. A warm feeling began to seep through him. He wondered what it would be like to be a stick of wood bouncing through the water, adrift but going somewhere. Where was he going? He forgot. He was just bobbing. It wasn't too bad. Why not stay?

He thought at first that the throbbing sound came from inside his head. Then he noticed a large object coming down from above, something whirling above it. Like the eddies in the rapids. Round and round and …

DAY TWELVE

3:16 PM

Calla finished her scheduled home visits. Another day of dutifully meeting her obligations, though she would be hard pressed to reconstruct what she had accomplished. Had it been less than two weeks since that late night call about Lonny? It felt like an eternity. One that wasn't over yet. Her thoughts constantly drifted back to the events on the rock overhang.

On her way to see Lonny at the hospital in Esterhill, she stopped at her apartment. She saw right away the dried grass just inside the door and dust everywhere. But after all that had happened, those imperfections didn't register in the same way they had before. She'd fix them eventually.

Since the ordeal, Lonny had been mostly mute, responding listlessly to questions with yes-or-no answers, but to little else. Only bruising remained from the physical ordeal; the real shock was in his mind. No one could diagnose how severe it might be. He was still undergoing tests, and there was a possibility that he might be transferred to Seattle for more specialized exams. For three days, he'd appeared completely unaware of where he was. Then he rebelled against the physical constraints of the hospital, throwing his food trays against the wall and refusing medication.

She thought she knew the basis of Lonny's behavior: he hated being cooped up anywhere. Next—and more difficult—was the pain of what Janice Casey had done to him. Yesterday a psychiatrist pressed him too far on that subject and he began to hit himself in the face.

What could be done with him? Lonny in an institution would be a slow death for both of them. The only difference was that hers would take longer. She couldn't afford the cost of long-term private therapy for him. And anyway, she really didn't believe that modern medicine could rescue Lonny. Not by itself. Modern methods worked only up to a point. The old remedies might be gentler, using a form of communication that Lonny understood, but they also might take longer. Right now, she had no viable alternative to hospitalization; and the thought of how long she might still have to be Lonny's caregiver led straight to her other heartache. Phil.

192

So many unexpected things had happened with him. After a long stretch of intense loneliness, here at last was someone she enjoyed spending time with, wanted to be with. There was nothing he could have done differently at the side of the river. She felt worse now than when she had yelled at him before taking off in the helicopter with Lonny. She had said ugly things, hurtful things, things that now embarrassed her to think about. Yet he still called every day, early and again late, never crowding her, just letting her know that he was there if she needed him. And what had she given him in return? Dull, uncommunicative responses.

She locked her apartment and tried to leave heavy thoughts behind as she drove to the hospital. Lonny was not in his room. A nurse pointed her to an outside door and an enclosed terrace beyond. There she saw a totally unexpected sight.

Bill McHugh was stretched out on a reclining wheel chair. One leg, in a hip-length cast, was elevated, and a casted arm rested on his chest in a sling. Oversized wrap-around dark glasses peeked out from under a baseball cap. Next to him a chair had been pulled up close, and in it sat Lonny, leaning toward McHugh. He didn't look away when he heard her approach.

He was too busy talking!

DAY THIRTEEN

6:43 AM

Phil awoke at first light. Of all the bright, beautiful mornings he'd seen out his window, this was the brightest, the most beautiful in a long, long time. He lifted a cup to his lips, feeling the warm coffee enter his throat, but hardly tasting it. The sunlit mountains before him, for all their grandeur, lacked detail. His mind was on last night.

Late yesterday afternoon he'd driven to Esterhill to visit Lonny and McHugh. He had planned only two hours for the drive and the visit. At first, everything worked out wrong: McHugh was unavailable, whisked away somewhere for more tests. And Lonny, the nurses told him, had a visitor. He'd checked his watch several times, conscious of the need to get back to Swiftwater. Finally, he peeked in. There was Calla, deep in conversation with Lonny.

A few minutes later, in the hallway, he and Calla spoke face to face for the first time since the river. He'd expected she would be brittle, desiccated, like her voice on the phone. Instead, color was in her cheeks and, though her demeanor reminded him of someone trying hard not to lose balance, a welcome vitality flitted in and out of her eyes. Conscious still of the difficult issues she had to face, he'd been careful, maybe too careful. She stopped in the middle of a sentence, observing him obliquely.

"I'm not eggs."

"What?"

A tentative laugh. Then an actual one.

"You don't have to watch your step that much."

He'd never heard anything more endearing.

She took a deep breath.

"And I'm really sorry for all those things I said. I didn't mean them, and I hope you can forgive me."

Of course he could! He'd dared a question, knowing it would probably be refused.

"How about dinner?"

She pretended mock conspiracy and her eyes amplified her smile.

"Your place or mine? No, wait ... yours. Mine's a mess."

He'd cooked and they'd talked, skirting any replay of the riverside events, though everything they mentioned was related in some way to them. He told her about the media attention that had started after police issued what they hoped would be a simple press release. There were lots of delicious tidbits in a story that combined murder, drugs, and a handicapped female mastermind. Every outlet found an angle for one lead. But this was Kittinach County, after all, and news from the population centers soon pushed the Janice story to the back pages, the end of the broadcasts, and out of the blogs. Instead of fighting a media firestorm, Phil spent many hours in dull meetings addressing what to do if the firestorm ever did occur.

He was lucky it never had come. He would have been useless; his mind had been locked on Calla all the time.

They'd talked about Lonny. Of course, Lonny. Calla knew the odds were slim for him, but she had gotten a huge lift from the way Lonny was reacting to McHugh. For the first time, Phil had heard connections between her tentative hopes for Lonny and possibilities for herself. For their new love, for the two of them together! Her words were like a bright bird on a perfect fir tree. You watched, but didn't move, so that brief moment wouldn't end.

They talked very little after that, left the dishes where they were, and went to the bedroom, as if that had been a mutual plan all along. Then they were in the bed, skin on skin, making love and exchanging loving words. Acts and words intermingled, played with each other, took on shapes and sounds that were entirely their own. Then they'd slept.

Calla was still sleeping soundly. But watching the landscape out the window come back into focus, he knew, for all the newness seeping through him, that there was no escaping a return to old reality.

He had to get back to being a better mayor than he'd been over the last half month. He'd skipped a lot; and even when present, he'd been present in body only. Fish or cut bait. All that had to change or he ought to look for another job.

In a while he'd be on his way to a promised meeting with Tom Cisek, then off to Esterhill to see Bill McHugh. Calla had an appointment with Lonny's primary physician at mid-morning, and Phil would meet her for lunch. In case today's details got lost in the rush of other emotions, he wrote a note and taped it to the kitchen counter, next to the freshly-made coffee.

Shortly after 7:30 he was in Cisek's spartan office. They swapped pleasantries, agreeing that it was high time to get back to normal. Phil couldn't miss Tom's seriousness on that issue. The Chief didn't pause before diving into a report about the negotiations on whether to charge Harland Casey, both at local and state levels.

"Once he knew that Janice wouldn't be around to take revenge, he began talking. Law enforcement in Arizona found the lab Casey described, and it turned out just like he said. So there's no reason to believe the drug operation was anything but Janice's. Besides, it's pretty obvious that Casey's no rocket scientist. Yesterday we brought him before a judge who heard reduced charges of vehicle theft, concealing evidence, and failure to cooperate with law enforcement. He got two years' probation. Now he goes back to Arizona to face possible charges of abetting a felon. But he might be all right. Far as we know, he stands to inherit any of Janice's property that's not tied to her drug activities. Could be a lot, could be a little; I'd guess the Feds will try to seize as much as they can. We're processing Casey for release right now. Want to say goodbye?"

"Why not?"

He found Casey in his cell, shaved and dressed, ready to go. Phil wished him well and meant it. He'd met other Harland Caseys, especially during his days as a reporter: men and women for whom life never went well, sometimes because of their own doings, but just as often for reasons beyond their control. In his heart, he had a soft spot for such unfortunate humans.

But when he held out a hand in parting, Casey all but spat on it.

"Save it. None of you believed me until you had to. I'm gone as soon as I'm outta here, trailer, truck and all. Maybe I'll get rich in Arizona, maybe not. But I'll survive, just like I've always had to. No thanks to people like you and the other fine upstanding citizens of Swiftwater."

A different look flashed across his face, as if he'd heard his own words and realized how thin and petty they sounded.

"But who the hell really cares?"

For a second, Phil glimpsed the frightened man behind the façade. Then Casey reinstalled his shell of bravado and turned away.

A half hour later, Phil parked in the hospital lot in Esterhill. When he inquired for Detective McHugh, he was directed to an outdoor terrace. Water for the raised flower and greenery beds had not yet evaporated from the slate tiles. Thin steam rose from them, predicting a hot and dry day ahead, matching the dun fields that spread out in the distance.

Funny, he thought, looking at the sere landscape; for a moment it all seemed green. But didn't everything look that way today?

He smiled, not caring who saw the look on his face.

10:00 AM

Jason watched Lila watching Jace as the little boy careened around new play equipment, then over and under the surrounding split-rail fence, before searching for a new route to do the whole trek over again. The kid's energy reminded Jason of how he had felt at that age. The difference was that he'd been punished for it. Little Jace was getting approval from his mom. And from his uncle.

Everything felt strange and good. The place was working out great. All three bedrooms were getting used. Lila kept everything immaculate. She was so good at it that he had stopped secretly looking around to spot what she'd missed. They'd bought food in bulk and filled the shelves and the big freezer, and could go for three weeks easy without a trip to town. Responding to an ad in the local Penny Saver, they'd visited a small organic farm a mile away where they found, as advertised, not only a floppy lab-mix puppy, but also two kids around Jace's age. Lila had taken Jace over there to play one afternoon, and was thinking about inviting the other kids to come here sometime soon.

Lila looked happier every day, new color on her face and a tiny smile at the edge of her mouth, like something she wanted to show but was still a little too shy—or afraid—to reveal. She didn't talk much, and never about the past. Except to say once that she never wanted to go back to drugs. He wondered how much her doing that depended on his staying close.

She had surprised him yesterday evening, saying that if he ever "found someone," she and Jace could move someplace else. He'd told her that there wasn't now, and wasn't likely to be, another person in his life. It got him thinking, though. Should he be looking around?

But then he remembered who he was and had been. Any looking around would have to wait a while. Laying low was a full-time business.

And he had another job that took up a few hours each day. An outbuilding was beginning to resemble his work room in Portal—ample broad tables, immaculately ordered shelves, and his two big computer screens glowing day and night. He was already online, selling products, placing ads, collecting commissions that added up little by little to real money. Not that he needed it. What he did need was a way of keeping his mind occupied.

He had stuck, and would continue to stick, with his resolve to stay out of the drug business. He genuinely hated the scene, the shifting unpredictability of it, the deals you could never trust, and, most of all, the lowlifes you had to hang out with. But he had to admit that, for all its messiness—actually, because of that—nothing matched it for complexity. For him, complexity was the narcotic, a state in which his mind, fully engaged, could paradoxically relax. He acknowledged this addiction, and he knew that flirting with it would lead directly back to the dangers had sworn to leave behind.

So he wouldn't think about that pleasure, he told himself; and thus avoid it. But he *was* thinking about it now. His Trojan horses were hoofing and snorting. His hands were itching, a sure sign. Maybe all he needed to do was destroy his backup devices and the information they contained, the way each day he promised himself he would.

He looked again at Lila and Jace, and at the idyllic mountain vistas on all sides, and enjoyed them fully.

So why was he also feeling a hint of ... desperation?

10:55 AM

Phil walked over to Greg, who sat beside Bill McHugh in a corner of the terrace. Greg pulled away from McHugh long enough to toss a quizzical look in Phil's direction.

"That smile mean you've got some good news?"

Phil was momentarily startled, and tried quickly to regain his usual neutral expression.

"Just enjoying the day."

He grabbed another metal patio chair to join the others.

Greg stared at him a little longer, then shrugged.

"Bill and I were talking about Harland Casey. Sounds like he might come out okay now that he's being released. Funny how you can almost like a guy when you know you can't really trust him."

At his elbow, McHugh regained some of his characteristic growl.

"You seem to make that a habit. Trusting the wrong people. Maybe something to watch out for."

Greg refused to let that slide.

"Meaning?"

McHugh, despite his cast, shifted his position and looked ready to hold his ground. A very large, bandaged bulldog.

"Ferris, too. Especially Ferris."

"I thought we were clear that he wasn't involved with Salvation or the murders. And clear about procedures even if he was."

McHugh's growl deepened.

"Being free of suspicion once doesn't make Ferris clean. He may have gone to ground, be holed up somewhere. But he'll be back. And when he does, I'll ..."

Phil cut him off. He had thought the easy conversation he saw when he first arrived meant that Greg and McHugh had worked things out between them. But they weren't all the way there, yet.

"Sounds like you fellows got a disagreement that needs some more private conversation. I've got other things to attend to so, if you don't mind, I want to ask Bill about something else."

Greg and McHugh exchanged a long stare. McHugh finally nodded and Phil went ahead.

"Okay. I've got to begin with a confession. Calla Ogden and I have gotten close recently."

McHugh's face lit up in a rare grin, his growl disappearing entirely.

"There's been rumors."

Phil grinned, too.

"Consider them confirmed. But…"

He gave his full attention to McHugh.

"…Lonny, even out of jail, is still a problem in need of a solution. The only difference is that now he's my problem, too."

He paused.

"Okay. Calla's convinced that Lonny will do poorly in any institution. Right or wrong, she believes that. Bill, Calla said you might have another idea."

McHugh's growl rumbled, but lost its threat—the voice of a man willing to show a different side of himself.

"Talking with Lonny here at the hospital reminded me of what I was like as a kid. I could have gone lots of bad ways. Toward drugs. Toward hating my life and myself. You know, all that. But I got turned in a better direction. Turned too much, maybe. Forgot what it's like to be Lonny. To be me, the way I was."

McHugh took a sip of water and looked into the distance.

"Lonny got off track on the Stick-shower stories. Made me mad. That Casey lady poisoned his mind. Most stories got nothin' to do with Stick-showers. There's lots of animals in them, some good, some bad. Humans do good things and bad. But Lonny's been filled with all of the bad."

When he continued, his gaze shifted briefly to his listeners, then back to the distance.

"I got this buddy up in Okanogan County, named Paul. Used to be a cop, and had to retire on disability. Like me, Paul's half Indian. He has a small group of boys and young men, all part Indian, all with big behavior problems. Some have done time. You get the picture?"

Phil nodded and saw Greg do the same.

"Well, Paul's put this program together slowly for about seven years. Gets some private donations, a little from BIA and the State.

Keeps it small on purpose. He wants only Indian youth, and knows that if the program gets too much notice it might be attacked on grounds of discrimination. You know, Native Americans getting preference, if that isn't a laugh."

More nods.

"Paul calls the group his tribe, and it's like one. He uses evenings in the high country to tell his kids about their heritage. But they also have to put out effort. They work in difficult places, clearing trails or removing underbrush in high-fire danger areas. That kind of thing. Weekends they go back to Paul's place, where he's converted an old building into a dorm. He's got teachers that come by. The idea is to get his kids back into regular education or employment. Sometimes it works, sometimes not. But Paul thinks it's better than tossing everyone in jail. So do I."

That was a long and revealing statement from someone who had built a reputation on short and gruff. Phil pressed him.

"And you think you can get Lonny in on that?"

"Maybe. Paul limits the group to fifteen, but he might squeeze in one more. See what I can do."

The answer was noncommittal, but he had no doubt McHugh would follow through. He was pretty sure his smile widened.

"We'd really appreciate it, Bill."

A nurse arrived and wheeled McHugh away, who gave a curt wave as a parting.

Greg stood and Phil did, too. Greg stacked their chairs.

"So it's 'we' now?"

"Getting there. Aw, shoot. Yeah, we're there. Why pretend different? But not much will happen until we get Lonny taken care of. What about you and Olga? Didn't you tell me she'd be coming for a visit?"

"Today, actually. I'm off in a few hours to SeaTac to pick her up."

"And how's all that going?"

"Ask me in a couple of days."

There was confidence in his tone, but Phil wondered whether Greg was any more sure than he was of what the future would bring.

They both would see.

3:17 PM

Calla finished her scheduled visit to a lake house located between Portal and Coho Corner. On the outside, the house wasn't any different from others in the cluster around it. Its exterior message to the world was that its inhabitants were doing well. In actuality, the family inside was in dire straits. An unemployed father watched TV all day while a mother of two small kids tried to find cheap food as their savings sank toward zero. Calla noted all the little signs that grim necessity was vanquishing what was left of the couple's pride. They already had to ask for food stamps and additional county assistance for the kids.

Back in her car, she noticed a missed call from an unidentified number. She drove a half mile to a turn-out with unobstructed line of sight to a cellular tower. Fir-clad mountains on both sides of a long, thin lake grew in height from the lake's lower end near Portal. To her right she could see the point where the lake ended at the entrance of a river descending from higher elevations. She glided her eyes across the panorama, letting nature expand and calm her senses. For a few minutes she basked in the lovely surroundings, inviting them to bathe away worries, hers and those she bore for others. Refreshed, she returned the missed call.

"Calla? Bill McHugh. Got something you might be interested in."

She listened to what he had to say, feeling a slow, warm joy start to spread inside of her. Lonny had been accepted into the troubled youth program; McHugh had made the arrangements. To her, the opportunity sounded hopeful. No, not just hopeful—it sounded right. There were no guarantees; but for the first time in years, Calla dared to believe that Lonny might find a way to live in which she would not have to be the sole provider.

She kept her eyes on the water and the mountains as she thanked McHugh and punched off. Their image expanded to match a buoyant feeling rising in her, like the release of a substance lighter than air into her lungs, into her heart. She was still grounded, but movement—simply raising her hand to touch her hair or holding it out the window to test the breeze—felt as light as it had once felt, years ago. Some invisible extra weight was sliding away.

For years she'd had an image of herself as an "in-between" person. At work, she got mostly the cases of people who, like her, were "in-between": between jobs, marriages, life periods, or cultures. She met them at a time when their past offered little support and the future looked bleak. She'd absorbed part of their rootlessness and pessimism; but now, she felt ready to see herself differently.

Though she had never let self-hate absorb her in the way it had absorbed and destroyed Janice Casey, her sense of being trapped had kept her from fully realizing the richness that life had given her. Having two cultures, living in two worlds, could be expanding, not constricting. Like living in nature. You got one view if you only looked down and saw the dirt, the dead leaves, and the broken twigs. You got another when you looked up and around, saw the water, the mountains, and the blue sky over everything.

As she could, right now.

She found the phone on the seat beside her and dialed a now familiar number.

"I want to be with you, Phil, and I'll be there as soon as I can,"

That's all she needed to say.

6:14 PM

Greg waited at the exit point of the A Concourse that emptied into the new wing of the Seattle-Tacoma airport. A replica of Charles Lindberg's *Spirit of Saint Louis* hung from the ceiling of a great hall. How could a plane so small have made it across the Atlantic Ocean? For that matter, who in the old USSR could have dreamed that two Ukrainians would be meeting each other in such a place as this?

At 5 pm, the airport was experiencing one of its busiest periods of the day; arriving passengers streamed by him and he worried that he might miss Olga. The surer alternative—meeting at baggage claim—had seemed too impersonal.

He could feel his elevated heartbeat driven both by happy anticipation and by apprehension about whether the passionate optimism that had filled them both their last time together had survived their time apart. In emails and occasional phone conversations, Olga had sounded so upbeat about the excitement of serving as a journalistic translator in Egypt that he wondered what in sleepy Central Washington could possibly match it. What in him could match it?

There she was! Tall, slim, blonde, her blue-green eyes brimming with anticipation and ... happiness?

Before he could do more than raise a hand, she had dropped her carry-on and flung her arms around his neck, holding her head back for a deep look into his eyes before she kissed him. His nagging worries evaporated.

When they paused to breathe, he could only manage two words. "You're here."

He said it in English. Back to their old dilemma: what language to use? She acknowledged in Russian, then grabbed his free hand as he lifted her bag with the other and began relating details of her trip in words that moved between Russian, Ukrainian, and English. By the time they got to baggage claim they were comfortably back in shifting, trilingual communication.

He had booked a room at a downtown Seattle hotel. The room had a balcony that afforded peek-a-boo glimpses of Puget Sound between the high surrounding buildings. But neither of them looked out the window. They dropped bags and without words fell together on the bed. Their lovemaking went from hasty to slow, becoming a full and delicious physical reunion. There was no remaining sign of the tentativeness of their first embrace, months ago. Everything was natural and as reassuring as it was deeply satisfying.

Following showers, a quiet shyness arrived that he recognized as their basically conservative natures responding to the uninhibited passion of just a few minutes before. They went up, hand in hand, to the rooftop terrace, where the day's warmth lingered and a slight breeze announced an overnight cooling. The sun was setting over the Olympic Mountains. While they waited for dinner, the sky above the Sound turned from washed-out light blue to a darker blue, then gray with pink-streaked clouds that faded gradually into nightfall. A waiter lit a miniature storm lantern on their table.

Sipping wine, they watched the transformation. As the sun disappeared, so did their ability to keep a conversation going with small talk alone. He didn't want to load down a pleasant time with heavier matters. But he also knew that avoiding those same matters was becoming a kind of heaviness in its own right. Someone had to start. He would.

"So you like your experience in Egypt."

She paused.

"Some parts of it."

"Which parts?"

Olga started her wine glass moving toward her mouth, but stopped before the rim touched her lips. The glass came down decisively.

"What you're really asking is whether I like Egypt better than Swiftwater. Whether I like independence more than I like being with you. Isn't that right?"

Part of what he loved about Olga was her ability—and her willingness—to confront most hard issues straight on, to look at reality instead of at its trappings. That attitude, however, carried the price of his having to respond in kind, something that was not easy for him. But he couldn't back out now.

"Yes, that's what I'm asking."

"And you want a complete answer right now?"

Her voice had risen. He reached across the table and covered her free hand.

"No, Olga. Tell me what you can."

Now he saw a conflicted look. She sighed.

"I knew we would have to have this talk. I thought maybe tomorrow."

"Okay, let's wait."

"No, you're right. Let's start."

Their food arrived and both of them had a chance to think. He thought about the inevitability of parting. What other answer could there be? When she was ready, Olga started, her eyes steadily on his, never looking away.

"You know why I accepted the Egypt job. Because one side of me wants to know the world, wants to be in the middle of big changes. That side of me is still there. It's strange: before I heard about the Egypt possibility, I would daydream about something like that coming along. When it did, I grabbed it. But do you know what I daydream about when I am in Egypt?"

He shook his head.

"The Cascades. Hikes in the woods. The peaceful pace of Swiftwater and Portal. And most of all, a life there with you."

His heart rose in flight, but he forced it to hover close by, not lift to where it wanted to go. There has to be a "but," he thought. He limited his response to a smile.

She smiled too, then reached for his other hand.

"I know myself well enough that I will always have to be active in the wider world. That doesn't mean all the time, or that I cannot have another, equally important part of my life. What scares me most in Egypt isn't the uncontrolled crowds, the chaos, or fanatic thugs. It's seeing many of the older female journalists. They are obsessed by events, but shriveled inside—unable, I imagine, to feel love. I didn't—I don't—want to become like that. Part of the answer to what I want depends on what you want. Can you live with and love someone who wants you, wants the best of Swiftwater but will also—and probably always—want something else, too?"

Now it was his turn to think. He could say, "It depends". Sure, any answer that reached very far into the future *did* depend on what she meant by involvement, on how he reacted to her choices, on how long Swiftwater continued to feel idyllic. But how far did they need to look ahead to find answers that mattered right now, tonight, tomorrow, and the next day? He let his heart respond.

"I love you as you are and as you want to be. The rest we'll discover by finding out how far that love takes us. By giving it a chance."

The light from the little lantern shone more brightly in her eyes. Or were those tears? They decided without a word to leave the rest of their dinner.

Back in the room, they made love again. Gradually, savoring sensations that had raced by them before, giving space for thoughts and feelings to unite.

The next morning they drove over Snoqualmie Pass, talking little, absorbing the panoramas and the soaring peaks of two national forests. When they descended on the eastern side, approaching Swiftwater and returning to signs of habitation, Olga spoke casually.

"You haven't told me about what kept you so busy and preoccupied over the last two weeks."

"Not much, really. You've had the more exciting life. Besides, I don't want to spoil your experience."

He pointed at the forested mountains on both sides of them.

She laughed.

"No place is perfect, except in imagination. We Ukrainians should know that. Your life is part of the world I explore. Besides, if we want the next two days to last, to become something more than just a visit, experiences we each have had should be ours together. Not yours. Not mine. Ours. So tell me."

And he did.

ACKNOWLEDGMENTS

Perhaps some authors do it all on their own. I'm not one of them, and as a result have leaned on others who have generously helped with personal support and professional advice.

Vernon Bogar II patiently introduced me to the history of the Yakama Nation and to the work done at the Cle Elum Supplementation and Research Facility (known locally as the "fish hatchery"). Vernon was also helpful in commenting on sections in the book that dealt with Yakama culture and history. Karen Bailey of Suncadia helped expand my knowledge of native plants.

For early comments and invaluable suggestions, I thank Margaret Amory and Roger Page.

Michael Neff took time off from his research to explain the equipment needed for drug analysis. An expert who wished to remain anonymous ("Deep Tech") helped with the details of computer and text message hacking. Richard Goodship offered important advice on police behavior. Finally. Claus and Pat, hard-working and honorable senior volunteers at the Cle Elum fish hatchery paradoxically, and through no fault of their own, gave me the idea for the polar-opposite characters who appear in this book. All these individuals also have my thanks.

Ghost Voices: Yakima Indian Myths, Legends, Humor, and Hunting Stories by Donald M. Hines was my primary source for the stories Calla tells or refers to. The "Pitpit Band" is fictional, though one tribe in the 1855 treaty with the Yakima Indians chose never to move to the Yakima reservation.

The names "Yakima" and Yakama" can cause confusion, and with reason. The treaty of 1855 was between the United States and the Yakima Indians, and there exist in Central Washington both a city and a river named "Yakima". In 1994, a new agreement was reached with the Federal Government which officially returned the spelling "Yakima" to its original "Yakama". The reservation near Toppenish, Washington and all official tribal matters are now under the Yakama Nation. Common parlance, however, still employs the term "Yakima". I chose to use throughout the book only the "Yakama" designation.

Adam Finley has once again been an imaginative and resourceful editor. Celeste Bennett has been supportive and helpful throughout the publishing process.

As always, this book, like previous endeavors, is better for the expert editorial assistance and personal encouragement of my wife Karen Neff. Any remaining mistakes are mine alone.

CBN

3/16/2012

CPSIA information can be obtained at www.ICGtesting.com
Printed in the USA
BVOW060041160512

290167BV00001B/7/P